THE LITTLE BIG BOOK OF
BASEBALL

THE LITTLE BIG BOOK OF
BASEBALL

EDITED BY HIRO CLARK WAKABAYASHI

DESIGNED BY JON GLICK

WELCOME BOOKS

NEW YORK · SAN FRANCISCO

TABLE OF CONTENTS

THE LITTLE BIG BOOK OF

BASEBALL

EDITED BY HIRO CLARK WAKABAYASHI

DESIGNED BY JON GLICK

WELCOME BOOKS
NEW YORK   SAN FRANCISCO

TABLE OF CONTENTS

FACTS

LEGENDS, LEAGUES & LORE

SPEECHES

INTRODUCTION

THIS BOOK REPRESENTS the twenty-fifth Little Big Book to appear in the Welcome series celebrating the people, places, and things we hold most dear in our lives: from moms, dads, grandmothers, and grandfathers to cats and dogs, laughter, marriage, America, and even Life itself. Not surprisingly, in this first Little Big Book devoted to a sport, it is to baseball, America's national pastime (as opposed to "favorite game"), that we pay homage.

Apart from the game itself and the playing of it in million-dollar stadiums, in sandlots, backyards, and streets across the country, even in small, enclosed playrooms where the lack of space is made up for by an abundance of dreaming and imagination, there is so much in our cultural history that honors baseball, and it has been both a challenge and a pleasure to search through it all and assemble this montage of words and pictures celebrating the game. I've filled this book not only with the legends of baseball (Ruth, Robinson, Aaron) and the classic moments (Bill Mazeroski's World Series–winning homer), but also with a wide range of lore and information, from the history of the Negro and Little Leagues to uniforms, from baseball in Japan to all the movies you shouldn't miss if you're a true fan. Then there are the many quotes from the likes of the eminently quotable Yogi Berra, the great speeches delivered by players and presidents, songs old and new, even favorite ballpark recipes, all of it brought vividly to life by nostalgic vintage art.

The Little Big Book of Baseball is, at its heart, a tribute to memory, for that is what the love of baseball is really all about. And underpinning the wide variety of artifacts collected here are the memories—true and imagined—of some of the greatest rememberers of our time: Plimpton, Kinsella, Angell, Barry, and Bryson, to name a few. All of these writers reach back in time, as well as into their own psyches, and draw forth a treasured tale or some special insight that reveals as much about their own love of the game as it does the particulars of their stories. In other words, it's personal. Baseball, like no other sport in America, is a personal matter.

We take it personally, I imagine, because most of us have played baseball or gone to the games, and we've learned from an early age to associate ourselves with the triumphs—or tribulations, as the case may be—of our favorite team and its players. From the anticipation of spring training and Opening Day in April to the climactic October battle between the long season's last two teams, baseball weaves its inexorable way into the fabric of our lives. With games being played almost every day through the summer, it forms a layer of our collective consciousness and provides a daily measure of our sense of place in the world. It isn't possible, really, to imagine a world without baseball. For me, it's a fact of existence that Derek Jeter will go crashing into the stands in pursuit of a foul ball, that Bernie Williams will deliver yet another clutch hit, and that the great Mariano Rivera will mow down with his cutter the last of the opposing team's hopes. These truths will never change, even with the passing of time and players into memory.

For all those fans with memories akin, this book's for you.

IT'S A GREAT DAY FOR A BALLGAME. LET'S PLAY TWO.
—ERNIE BANKS

TAKE ME OUT TO THE BALLGAME:
BALLPARK TRIVIA

☆ The first known baseball park was built in 1862 for Brooklyn's Union Club, by William Cammeyer.

☆ The Kansas City Royals' Kauffman Stadium showcases a 322-foot-wide water "spectacular that comprises one of the largest privately funded fountain systems in the world."

☆ "The Safe"—Seattle's Safeco Field, constructed in 1999 cost $517.6 million to build and has a one-of-a-kind retractable roof that weighs 22 million pounds.

☆ Opened in 1912, Boston's Fenway Park is the oldest ballpark still in operation.

☆ The first major-league game to take place under the lights was at Cincinnati's Crosley Field in 1935, when the Reds played the Phillies. President Franklin D. Roosevelt ceremonially turned on the lights from the White House.

☆ Minnesota's Metrodome, Tampa Bay's Tropicana Field, and Toronto's Rogers Centre are the only stadiums that use artificial turf instead of real grass.

12

★ The deepest outfield wall, coming in at 436 feet from home plate, is at Houston's Minute Maid Park. The field also features the world's largest sliding glass door, in left field. It's 50,000 square feet and hurricane-proof.

★ At Wrigley Field, if a ball gets caught in the ivy, it counts as a ground rule double.

★ Tampa Bay's Tropicana Field has a restaurant that seats 350 people in center field, but is invisible to hitters due to its special glass coating.

★ Yankee Stadium was the first ballpark to be called a stadium.

★ The Ameriquest Field in Arlington, Texas, features a field built 22 feet below street level to avoid seasonal winds.

★ A single row of purple seats wraps around the upper deck of Coors Field in Denver, marking one mile above sea level.

★ L.A.'s Dodger Stadium, in keeping with its reputation for cleanliness, gets repainted every year.

★ The hot summer sun played a big role in the design of the Diamondbacks' Bank One Ballpark. Its nine-million-pound roof can retract in less than five minutes. There is also a luxurious seating area—the Sun Pool Party Pavilion—where 35 guests can watch the game from the cool comfort of a swimming pool.

★ If you hit a home run over the right wall of San Francisco's SBC Park, your ball will go straight into San Francisco Bay. Beyond the wall is McCovey Cove, named for the Giants' Hall of Famer Willie McCovey.

- The Athletics' McAfee Coliseum, formerly Oakland-Alameda County Coliseum, was where the crowd-pleasing activity known as the Wave made its first known appearance in baseball on October 15, 1981.

- Team history is often honored at ballparks. The Angels have a statue of Gene Autry; the Brewers created a Walk of Fame; the Reds immortalized Stan Musial; and the Braves have a Monument Grove.

- At Shea Stadium's opening ceremonies in 1964, Bill Shea christened the new park with water from the Gowanus Canal near Ebbets Field and water from the Harlem River near the Polo Grounds.

- Oriole Park at Camden Yards is two blocks from Babe Ruth's birthplace. Center field is now located on the site of the Ruth's Café, Babe's father's old restaurant.

- The Pirates' PNC Park has a 21-foot right-field wall in honor of Roberto Clemente, who wore the number 21.

- Comerica Park features a Ferris wheel with cars shaped like baseballs and a carousel with 30 hand-painted tigers.

- At the Phillies' Citizens Bank Park, kids can make their own stuffed mascot Phanatic at the Build-a-Bear workshop.

- The White Sox's U.S. Cellular Field provides "Rain Rooms" for its fans; these emit a cool mist on hot summer days.

- The Cleveland Indians had to play in a stadium nicknamed "the Mistake by the Lake" for more than 60 years. But since 1994, the team has enjoyed Jacobs Field, an asymmetrical ballpark that offers great views of the downtown skyline.

- At San Diego's new PETCO Park, the left-field foul pole is part of a San Diego landmark, the Western Metal Supply building.

Shea Stadium, New York, New York

Honey-Roasted Peanuts

4 cups peanuts

¼ cup honey

¼ cup vegetable
or peanut oil

¼ cup water

½ cup sugar

1 teaspoon salt

Have you ever smelled anything better than warm honey-roasted peanuts? Having a bowl of them in front of your guests during the game will make everyone feel a part of the action on screen—but beware, they might all be gone by the bottom of the first.

1. Preheat the oven to 350 degrees.

2. Place the peanuts on a cookie sheet and into the oven. Bake until lightly browned, stirring occasionally (5 to 10 minutes).

3. Remove from the oven and set aside.

4. On the stove, bring the honey, oil, and water to a boil. Add the peanuts and stir until all the liquid has been absorbed.

5. In a bowl, mix the sugar and salt. Add the peanut-honey mixture.

6. Spread the honey-roasted peanuts out on waxed paper to cool.

Serves 4 to 6.

THE FRONT LINES TO THE BACKYARD

BY TOM BROKAW

For all of the recent challenges to the claim that baseball is our national pastime, no other sport touches the chord of patriotism in quite the same way.

Why is that? Some of the Super Bowl halftime shows have been extravagant appeals to pride in America. And who could forget the image of the U.S. Olympic hockey team members draped in the American flag following their "miracle on ice" at the 1980 winter games? Yet baseball, much more than the other sports, has that Yankee-Doodle dandy, it's a grand old flag, from sea to shining sea, rockets' red glare kind of feeling.

I think there are several reasons. It was during World War I that baseball games became a kind of pep rally for the boys who were over there, fighting the war that was supposed to end all wars. Francis Scott Key's anthem was installed as a pregame fixture during that time. Red, white, and blue bunting decorated the ballparks.

By the time the United States got involved in World War II, baseball was indisputably a national obsession. While professional basketball and pro football were struggling to get established, major league baseball was deeply rooted in the American psyche. Families thousands of miles from big league cities were known by the team for which they rooted or the player who won their lasting loyalty. Radio broadcasts of important games, especially the World Series, were practically national holidays.

So when major leaguers were drafted or they volunteered for military service it was a Movietone moment, a highlight of the newsreels that played in every movie theater in the country. The biggest stars—Joe DiMaggio, Ted Williams, Hank Greenberg, Bob Feller—were all in uniform. No recruiting poster or piece of government propaganda could equal the effect of these baseball heroes giving up the prime years of their careers to serve their country. Williams, in fact, devoted four and a half seasons in the prime of his career to military service, in both World War II and Korea. He wasn't doing desk duty, either. He was using his perfect vision and perfectionistic work ethic to fly fighter planes.

In the movies, when American G.I.s wanted to trick a German posing as an American, they'd ask a baseball question. "You're from the States, huh? So who did you like in the '41 Series?"

In the end, baseball has an enduring connection to the idea of America because it is really an extension of democracy. It is played in all of the levels of our national life, from small town to big city, from the reservation to the barrio, from manicured suburban fields to rocky pastures.

In its most elemental form, there's room for all, whatever their athleticism, ethnicity, or economic status. The fabric of America can be found in a pick-up game with a granddad umpiring, a fat kid in right field, a woman at the plate, a cheering section of relatives, and strangers who wander by, unable to resist the spectacle of so many people having so much fun.

If there's any further doubt, remember the final two words in our national anthem: "Play ball!"

Well—it's our game; that's the chief fact in connection with it; America's game; it has the snap, go, fling of the American atmosphere; it belongs as much to our institutions; fits into them as significantly as our Constitution's laws; is just as important in the sum total of our historic life.

—Walt Whitman

GREAT MOMENTS
IN BASEBALL PART I

July 16, 1941 Joe DiMaggio safely hits in his 56th straight game, a record that still stands (above).

September 28, 1941 Ted Williams of the Boston Red Sox finishes the season with a .406 batting average, the last player to do so.

October 15, 1946 Cardinal Enos Slaughter makes his "Mad Dash" from first all the way home off a double from Harry Walker, thus ensuring a World Series victory over the Red Sox.

October 3, 1951 The New York Giants win the pennant after Bobby Thomson hits a long drive into the stands, commonly referred to as "the Shot Heard 'Round the World."

September 29, 1954 Willie Mays of the New York Giants makes an unforgettable full-speed catch, also known as "The Catch," over his left shoulder to hold the win over the Indians during Game 1 of the World Series.

October 3, 1955 In the sixth inning of Game 7 of the World Series between the New

York Yankees and Brooklyn Dodgers, Sandy Amoros catches Yogi Berra's fly ball and rockets it infield to Pee Wee Reese, who fires it to first base for a double play, ending the Yankees' rally and clinching the World Series victory for Brooklyn.

October 8, 1956 Yankee Don Larsen pitches the only perfect game in World Series history, against the Dodgers.

May 26, 1959 Pirate Harvey Haddix pitches 12 perfect innings against the Milwaukee Braves until Felix Mantilla reaches base on an error which results in Hank Aaron being intentionally walked. Then Milwaukee first baseman Joe Adcock hits a home run, ending one of the most spectacular pitching performances in history.

October 13, 1960 In the ninth inning of Game 7 of the 1960 World Series between the New York Yankees and the Pittsburgh Pirates, Bill Mazeroski becomes the first player to end a World Series with a home run.

October 1, 1961 Yankee Roger Maris hits a fastball into the right-field seats of Yankee Stadium to become the single-season home run king, with 61 homers (below).

October 3, 1951
The New York Giants celebrate winning
the pennant after Bobby Thomson hits
a long drive into the stands.

Slide, Kelly, Slide!

BY J. W. KELLY

I play'd a game of baseball,
I belong to Casey's Nine!
The crowd was feeling jolly,
And the weather it was fine;

A nobler lot of players,
I think were never found.
When the omnibuses landed
That day upon the ground,

The game was quickly started,
They sent me to the bat:
I made two strikes, says Casey,
"What are you striking at?"

I made the third, the Catcher muff'd,
And to the ground it fell;
Then I run like a divil to first base,
When the gang began to yell:

Slide, Kelly, slide!
Your running's a disgrace!
Slide, Kelly, slide!
Stay there, hold your base!

If someone doesn't steal you,
And your batting doesn't fail you,
They'll take you to Australia!
Slide, Kelly, slide!

'Twas in the second inning
They call'd me in, I think,
To take the catcher's place, while
He went to get a drink;

But something was the matter,
Sure I couldn't see the ball;
And the second one that came in,
Broke my muzzle, nose and all.

The crowd up in the Grand Stand,
They yelled with all their might;
I ran towards the Club House,
I thought there was a fight.

'Twas the most unpleasant feeling,
I ever felt before;
I knew they had me rattled,
When the gang began to roar:

Slide, Kelly, slide!
Your running's a disgrace!
Slide, Kelly, slide!
Stay there, hold your base!

If someone doesn't steal you,
And your batting doesn't fail you,
They'll take you to Australia!
Slide, Kelly, slide!

They sent me out to centrefield,
I didn't want to go;
The way my nose was swelling up,
I must have been a show!

29

They said on me depended
Vict'ry or defeat.
If a blind man was to look at us,
He'd know that we were beat.

"Sixty four to nothing!"
Was the score when we got done,
And ev'rybody there but me,
Said they had lots of fun.

The news got home ahead of me,
They heard I was knock'd out;
The neighbors carried me in the house,
And then began to shout:

Slide, Kelly, slide!
Your running's a disgrace!
Slide, Kelly, slide!
Stay there, hold your base!

If someone doesn't steal you,
And your batting doesn't fail you,
They'll take you to Australia!
Slide, Kelly, slide!

The Kid

E. Ethelbert Miller

about the second month of the season
we start catching word about the kid
talk about strikeouts and shutouts
how his curve breaks and his fastball smokes
frank and i were driving trucks up in the mountains
listening to the games
betting our wages and drinking beer
we get the newspapers each morning and check the standings
frank is a giants fan
been that way since the day willie mays broke in
that was the same year his father died
in an accident on the highway three days before christmas
sometimes when we ain't talking about baseball
frank will talk about his father
talk about him the way some folks be talking about the kid

President Calvin Coolidge

October 1, 1924, White House Lawn

They are a great band, these armored knights of the bat and ball. They are held up to a high standard of honor on the field, which they have seldom betrayed. While baseball remains our national game, our national tastes will be on a higher level and our national ideals on a finer foundation.

TY COBB

ONE OF THE MOST PROLIFIC hitters in the game, Ty Cobb batted under .300 only once in his career. His reputation as a disagreeable man never diminished his superstar status. He always, more than anything, wanted to win. Born December 18, 1886, as Tyrus Raymond Cobb, Ty was raised by a well-educated father who demanded that his son succeed in life. Intending to become a Georgia politician, like his father, or a physician, Ty was sidetracked by his own talent for athletics.

In 1905, Cobb became an outfielder for the Detroit Tigers at the age of 18. He soon developed an intimidating playing style, pushing himself to extremes to come out ahead. He would not only play with a 103° fever, but steal three bases and get three hits in the process. He studied pitchers and discovered their weaknesses. In the off-season, he hunted with weighted boots and practiced sliding until his legs were raw. Cobb's work paid off. In 1907, he won his first of 12 batting titles and helped bring the Tigers to the World Series.

His achievements at the plate are unmatched even today. In 1911, his batting average was .420, and in his 24 seasons, he batted over .300 in 23, compiling a lifetime average of .366, the highest for any player. At 24, he was the youngest player to reach the 1,000-hit mark. He led the game in runs scored for 70 years and hits for 60 years. Cobb's speed was another of his strengths. From first base he stole second, third, and home six times in his career, with a total of 96 stolen bases in 1915 alone. The only thing that ever eluded the Georgia Peach was a World Series victory. Though his teams were always very competitive, the Tigers' three trips to the championships never ended with a win.

In his last playing seasons, Ty Cobb also managed the Tigers. Signing him in that position surprised most people, as Cobb lacked the people skills generally associated with a manager. The players on the team respected him, but certainly did not like him, and this feeling increased with Cobb as the manager. He demanded from his players the same effort that he put into each game, and was always disappointed. In 1926, Cobb found himself in the midst of a gambling scandal. Though he was cleared of any wrongdoing, Cobb quit the Tigers and signed with the Philadelphia A's in 1927, only to retire a year later.

When his career finally ended, Cobb held an impressive number of records: most at-bats, hits, stolen bases, runs, and lifetime batting average. He started to invest, putting his money in Coca-Cola, a company that would make him a multimillionaire. With his earnings, he endowed several hospitals in Georgia, now known as the Ty Cobb Healthcare System. In 1936, Ty was inducted into the Hall of Fame as one of the "First Five"; Cobb received the most votes of all. On July 17, 1961, he passed away in Georgia surrounded by his family and first wife.

BASEBALL IS NINETY PERCENT MENTAL, THE OTHER HALF IS PHYSICAL.

—YOGI BERRA

WACKY BUT TRUE

★ Lou Novikoff, an outfielder for the Cubs in the '40s, refused to go back to the wall to catch balls hit by opposing teams because of his "fear of vines." Vines, of course, cover the back wall of Wrigley Field.

★ As a game was starting in Toronto in 1983, Yankees outfielder Dave Winfield threw a warm-up ball off the field, hitting a low-flying seagull (which was looking for dropped popcorn) and instantly killing it. He was charged with a $500 fine for cruelty to animals, but the charges were later dropped.

★ "Ashburn Ridge" at Connie Mack Stadium in Philadelphia was an interesting (and illegal) creation by the groundskeeping team. Phillie Richie Ashburn was an excellent bunter, so the team planted a slight ridge of grass along the third-base foul line, ensuring his hits stayed fair, and Ashburn won the 1955 and 1958 batting titles.

★ The Giants cheated during their pennant-winning 1951 season. A coach hid in the center-field clubhouse with a telescope aimed at the opposing team's catcher while the Giants were at bat. Another Giant sat on the bullpen bench in deep right-center field listening for a bell or a buzzer from the coach that identified the next pitch, which he then signaled to the batter.

☆ On July 15, 1973, Angel Nolan Ryan pitched his second no-hitter of the season against the Tigers in Detroit, prompting Tiger Norm Cash to come to the plate with two outs in the ninth holding a table leg instead of a bat. Umpire Ron Luciano, laughing heartily, made Cash use a real bat for his pop fly, which ended the game.

☆ In 1951, Johnny Neves from the Northern League Fargo-Moorhead Twins wore his number 7 backward on his jersey— because his last name spelled backward is *seveN*.

☆ The actor Jack Webb from *Dragnet* was a huge baseball fan. His character, Sergeant Joe Friday, carried the shield number 714— his way of honoring Babe Ruth and his 714 career home runs.

☆ In 1989, the Pittsburgh Pirates were up 10–0 against the Phillies in Philadelphia when Pirate announcer and former pitcher Jim Rooker swore he'd walk back to Pittsburgh if the Pirates lost the game. They did, and Rooker walked over 300 miles home following the season— raising $81,000 for charity as he went.

☆ The Chicago Cubs believe they were cursed by a billy goat. In 1945, Bill Sianas and Murphy, his baseball-loving goat, tried to enter the World Series at Wrigley Field. When they were turned away for fear the goat would smell too bad, Bill cursed the team. The Cubs lost, and have continued to do so ever since.

San Diego Padres' Fish Tacos

FISH

12 fresh cod fillets

12 corn tortillas

1 head of cabbage, shredded

6 limes, quartered

WHITE SAUCE

½ cup mayonnaise

½ cup plain yogurt

2 tablespoons cilantro, chopped

BEER BATTER

1 cup flour

1 cup dark beer

½ teaspoon garlic salt

pepper to taste

San Diego's PETCO Park is known for its Mahi Mahi fish tacos, served up with a side of rice and beans. If you can't make it to sunny San Diego, you can still enjoy fantastic fish tacos with outstanding pico de gallo. Fresh, mild, and crispy to perfection, these tacos are a Southern California staple.

1. Begin by cleaning fish in a large bowl of cold, salted water. Pat fish dry, and dice into 1-to-2-inch cubes.

2. In a small serving bowl, combine mayonnaise, yogurt, and cilantro. Place in refrigerator to chill.

3. In another serving bowl, combine tomatoes, garlic, onion, cilantro, lime juice, and jalapeño. Add salt and pepper to taste. Set aside.

4. In a small skillet, lightly warm tortillas.

5. In a large, heavy skillet or deep-fat fryer, place enough vegetable oil to completely submerge fish pieces. Heat oil to 375° F.

6. Combine flour, beer, and spices, stirring until well-incorporated.

7. Dunk fish cubes into batter and fry in a single layer, turning as needed to achieve a uniform, golden-brown crispiness. Repeat until all the fish is cooked.

8. Lightly sprinkle with salt and lime juice as fish is taken out of oil.

PICO DE GALLO

6 tomatoes, diced

2 cloves
garlic, minced

½ onion, diced

2 tablespoons
cilantro, chopped

juice of 1 lime

2 jalapeño peppers,
seeded and chopped
(It is best to use
rubber gloves
when handling hot
peppers. If you
choose not to use
gloves, please
exercise caution.)

salt and pepper
to taste

vegetable oil
for frying

lime juice

salt

9. Assemble each taco by layering a warm tortilla with white sauce, shredded cabbage, several fish cubes, and pico de gallo. Serve with limes and hot sauce.

Serves 6.

OUR NATIONAL PASTIME

BY DAVE BARRY

As I ponder the start of yet another baseball season, what is left of my mind drifts back to the fall of 1960, when I was a student at Harold C. Crittenden Junior High ("Where the Leaders of Tomorrow Are Developing the Acne of Today").

The big baseball story that year was the World Series between the New York Yankees and the Pittsburgh Pirates. Today, for sound TV viewership reasons, all World Series games are played after most people, including many of the players, have gone to bed. But in 1960 the games had to be played in the daytime, because the electric light had not been invented yet. Also, back then the players and owners had not yet discovered the marketing benefits of sporadically canceling entire seasons.

46

The result was that in those days young people were actually interested in baseball, unlike today's young people, who are much more interested in basketball, football, soccer and downloading dirty pictures from the Internet. But in my youth, baseball ruled. Almost all of us boys played in Little League, a character building experience that helped me develop a personal relationship with God.

"God," I would say, when I was standing in deep right field—the coach put me in the right field only because it was against the rules to put me in Sweden, where I would have done less damage to the team—"please please PLEASE don't let the ball come to me."

But of course God enjoys a good prank as much as the next infallible deity, which is why, when He heard me pleading with Him, He always took time out from His busy schedule to make sure the next batter hit a towering blast that would, upon re-entering the Earth's atmosphere, come down directly where I would have been standing, if I had stood still, which I never did. I lunged around cluelessly in frantic, random circles, so that the ball always landed a minimum of 40 feet from where I wound up standing, desperately thrusting out my glove, which was a Herb Score model that, on my coach's recommendation, I had treated with neat's-foot oil so it would be supple. Looking back, I feel bad that innocent neats had to sacrifice their feet for the sake of my glove. I would have been just as effective, as a fielder, if I'd been wearing a bowling shoe on my hand, or a small aquarium.

But even though I stunk at it, I was into baseball. My friends and I collected baseball cards, the kind that came in a little pack with a dusty, pale-pink rectangle of linoleum-textured World War II surplus bubble gum that was far less edible than the cards themselves. Like every other male my age who collected baseball cards as a boy, I now firmly believe that at one time I had the original rookie cards of Mickey Mantle, Jackie Robinson, Ty Cobb, Babe Ruth, Jim Thorpe, Daniel Boone, Goliath, etc., and that I'd be able to sell my collection for $163 million today except my mom threw it out.

My point is that we cared deeply about baseball back then, which meant that we were passionate about the 1960 Pirates–Yankees World Series matchup. My class was evenly divided between those who were Pirate fans and those who were complete morons. (I never have cared for the Yankees, and for a very sound reason: The Yankees are evil.)

We followed every pitch of every game. It wasn't easy, because the weekday games started when we were still in school, which for some idiot reason was not called off for the World Series. This meant that certain students—I am not naming names, because even now, it could go on our Permanent Records—had to carry concealed transistor radios to class. A major reason why the Russians got so far ahead of us, academically, during the Cold War is that while Russian students were listening to their teachers explain the cosine, we were listening, via concealed earphones, to announcers explain how a bad hop nailed Tony Kubek in the throat.

That Series went seven games, and I vividly remember how it ended. School was out for the day, and I was heading home, pushing my bike up a steep hill, listening to my cheapo little radio, my eyes staring vacantly ahead, my mind locked on the game. A delivery truck came by, and the driver stopped and asked if he could listen. Actually, he more or less told me he was going to listen; I said OK.

The truck driver turned out to be a rabid Yankee fan. The game was very close, and we stood on opposite sides of my bike for the final two innings, rooting for opposite teams, him chain-smoking Lucky Strike cigarettes, both of us hanging on every word coming out of my tinny little speaker.

And of course if you were around back then and did not live in Russia, you know what happened: God, in a sincere effort to make up for all those fly balls he directed toward me in

Little League, had
Bill Mazeroski—
Bill Mazeroski!—hit
a home run to win it
for the Pirates.

I was insane with
joy. The truck driver
was devastated. But I will
never forget what he said to
me. He looked me square
in the eye, one baseball fan
to another, after a tough but fair
fight—and he said a seriously
bad word. Several, in fact.
Then he got in his truck
and drove away.

That was the best
game I ever saw.

BASEBALL IS LIKE
CHURCH: MANY ATTEND,
FEW UNDERSTAND.

—WES WESTRUM

Tally One for Me

BY JOHN T. RUTLEDGE

I'm the pride and pet of all the girls
That come out to the park,
My ev'ry play out in the field,
You bet they're sure to mark.

And when you see them smiling and
Their hands go pit-a-pat,
Just mark it down, for number one
Is going to the bat, oh!

For when I take the bat in hand
My style is sure and free…
Just put your money on my side,
And tally one for me…

I never knock the ball up high,
Or even make it bound,
But always send it whizzing,
Cutting daises in the ground.

I always make a clean base hit,
And go around you see,
And that's the reason why I say
Just tally one for me, oh!

For when I take the bat in hand
My style is sure and free...
Just put your money on my side,
And tally one for me...

I soon will stop my "balling,"
For my heart is led astray,
'Twas stolen by a nice young girl,
By her exquisite play.

And after we are married, why,
I hope you'll come to see,
The "tally" I have made for life,
And mark it down for me, oh!

For when I take the bat in hand
My style is sure and free...
Just put your money on my side,
And tally one for me...

From Pantaloons to Pinstripes:
Uniform Style

☆ In 1849, the New York Knickerbockers adopted an official uniform that consisted of blue woolen pantaloons, white flannel shorts, and straw hats.

☆ The Cincinnati Red Stockings changed their uniform from pantaloons to knickers in 1868, for the sake of comfort.

☆ Team names first showed up on belts, not shirts, with Brooklyn's Excelsiors leading the way in 1860.

☆ Wool was originally used in uniforms because the fabric separated the clubs from the working class, who could only afford cotton. Some teams even wore ties to look more distinguished.

☆ The 1882 rules required each player to wear a different color depending on his position. Only stocking color associated a player with his team.

☆ The Old English–style logo of the Detroit Tigers is the oldest major-league motif still used today.

☆ The stitched visor on the baseball cap was added in 1903 to create longer-lasting headgear.

☆ Numbers weren't put on uniforms until 1907, when Pennsylvania's Reading Red Roses wore the numbers 1 through 14 (with 13 being left out for superstitious reasons). Other clubs did not adopt the idea until 1932.

☆ The Yankees have worn their famous pinstripes every season since 1915.

☆ The 1938 All-Star Game featured Ted Williams, Eddie Joost, and blue satin uniforms that shone under the lights. Other clubs soon began using this attention-getting fabric for night games as well, but the trend did not last.

☆ To celebrate the nation's Bicentennial and the National League "Senior Circuit's" 100th anniversary in 1976, several teams wore pillbox-style caps. The Pirates liked the look so much, they kept the hats until 1986.

☆ The first retired number was Lou Gehrig's 4, retired by the Yankees in 1939. Now more than 100 major league players have had their numbers retired by their teams.

☆ Jackie Robinson's number 42 was retired from all of baseball in 1997, meaning no player in the major or minor leagues can ever again wear 42.

4 42

☆ To honor America and its heroes, the uniform has often been adapted to the times. In World War II, jerseys incorporated a patriotic patch in the shape of a shield; after September 11, an American flag patch was sewn on the back of each jersey, as well as one on each cap.

☆ The 2002–2006 Collective Bargaining Agreement is the first in major-league history to include uniform regulations. It contains seven regulations regarding pants alone!

COOL PAPA BELL was said to be the fastest man in baseball. Josh Gibson's home runs were legendary. Buck Leonard terrorized pitchers with his powerful swing. Each one is a member of the National Baseball Hall of Fame, and each one was denied the right to play in the major leagues because of the color of his skin. They,

THE NEGRO LEAGUES

along with hundreds of other men in the Negro Leagues, gave a community something to cheer about for more than 50 years.

In 1890, the International League banned African American players from baseball. Though few black players had been allowed in the majors before, this new law left a hole for athletes in the African American community. Many all-black teams formed and took barnstorming tours throughout the country. The first real organization came in 1920 when Andrew "Rube" Foster, a pitcher and owner of the Chicago American Giants, gathered owners in the Midwest to form the Negro National League. Other formal leagues followed, including the Negro Southern and Eastern Leagues. Then in 1924, the first Negro World Series was held, with the Kansas City Monarchs winning the championship.

The fall of the stock market caused problems for the leagues, especially with most of their paying fans out of work. One by one, the leagues crumbled. Eventually, a new National League was formed, with a new All-Star Game featuring famous players like Satchel Paige, Josh Gibson, and Martín Dihigo. The game became the biggest black sporting event, drawing 20,000 to 30,000 fans every year through the '30s and '40s.

During regular league play, two teams became the best in the business: the Homestead Grays and the Kansas City Monarchs. The Monarchs won five of the six first Negro League Championships and featured the unstoppable pitching arm of Paige. The Grays were the team everyone wanted to beat, but never could. On their roster were Gibson and Leonard, "the twin twisters," who helped the Grays win nine straight championships.

The downfall of the Negro Leagues came after almost sixty years of segregation, when the Brooklyn Dodgers signed Jackie Robinson in 1946. The next year, the Cleveland Indians signed Larry Doby, and then, a year later, Paige as well. Paige became the oldest major-league rookie at the age of 42. Within six years of the color barrier being broken, the last Negro League folded. The end was inevitable once more than 150 former players signed on to major-league teams and left the Negro Leagues' rosters depleted of star talent. The new battle was in the majors, where black players had to fight through adverse conditions to be accepted as team members.

In the end, the Negro Leagues not only supported the emotional well-being of the black community, but also helped to build economic foundations. They provided an opportunity for men to excel and demonstrate their skill on a national level through 11 World Series and 15 All-Star Games. But most of all, they created a sense of hope for African Americans at a time when there was very little to hope for.

Catfish

WORDS BY BOB DYLAN
& JACQUES LEVY
MUSIC BY BOB DYLAN

Lazy stadium night
Catfish on the mound
"Strike three," the umpire said
Batter have to go back and sit down

Catfish
Million dollar man
Nobody can throw the ball
Like Catfish can

Used to work on Mr. Finley's farm
But the old man wouldn't pay
So he packed his glove and took his arm
An' one day he just ran away

Catfish
Million dollar man
Nobody can throw the ball
Like Catfish can

Come up where The Yankees are
Dress up in a pin-stripe suit
Smoke a custom-made cigar
Wear an alligator boot

Catfish
Million dollar man
Nobody can throw the ball
Like Catfish can

Carolina born and bred
Love to hunt the little quail
Got a hundred-acre spread
Got some huntin' dogs for sale

Catfish
Million dollar man
Nobody can throw the ball
Like Catfish can

Reggie Jackson at the plate
Seein' nothin' but the curve
Swing too early or too late
Got to eat what Catfish serve

Catfish
Million dollar man
Nobody can throw the ball
Like Catfish can

Even Billy Martin grins
When the Fish is in the game
Every season twenty wins
Gonna make the Hall of Fame

Catfish
Million dollar man
Nobody can throw the ball
Like Catfish can

To Satch

Samuel Allen

Sometimes I feel like I will *never* stop

Just go on forever

Till one fine mornin'

I'm gonna reach up and grab me a

    handfulla stars

Swing out my long lean leg

And whip three hot strikes burnin'

    down the heavens

And look over at God and say,

How about that!

AGE IS A QUESTION OF
MIND OVER MATTER.
IF YOU DON'T MIND,
IT DOESN'T MATTER.
—SATCHEL PAIGE

IT WAS A GREAT DAY IN JERSEY

BY WENDELL SMITH
APRIL 18, 1946, *PITTSBURGH COURIER*

Jersey City, N. J.—The sun smiled down brilliantly in picturesque Roosevelt Stadium here Thursday afternoon and an air of excitement prevailed throughout the spacious park, which was jammed to capacity with 25,000 jabbering, chattering opening day fans... A seething mass of humanity, representing all segments of the crazy-quilt we call America, poured into the magnificent ball park they named after a man from Hyde Park—Franklin D. Roosevelt—to see Montreal play Jersey City and the first two Negroes in modern baseball history perform, Jackie Robinson and Johnny Wright... There was the usual fanfare and color, with mayor Frank Hague chucking out the first ball, the band music, kids from Jersey City schools putting on an exhibition of running, jumping and acrobatics... There was also the hot dogs, peanuts and soda pop... And some guys in the distant bleachers whistled merrily: "Take Me Out to the Ball Game"... Wendell Willkie's "One World" was right here on the banks of the Passaic River.

The outfield was dressed in a gaudy green, and the infield was as smooth and clean as a new-born babe... And everyone sensed the significance of the occasion as Robinson and Wright marched with the Montreal team to deep centerfield for the raising of the Stars and Stripes and the "Star-Spangled Banner"... Mayor Hague strutted proudly with his henchmen flanking him on the right and left... While the two teams, spread across the field, marched side by side with military precision and the band played on... We all stood up—25,000 of us—when the band struck up the National Anthem... And we sang lustily and freely, for this was a great day... Robinson and Wright stood out there with the rest of the players and dignitaries, clutching their blue-crowned baseball caps, standing erect and as still as West Point cadets on dress parade.

WHAT WERE THEY THINKING ABOUT?

No one will ever know what they were thinking right then, but I have traveled more than 2,000 miles with their courageous pioneers during the past nine weeks—from Sanford, Fla., to Daytona Beach to Jersey City—and I feel that I know them probably better than any newspaperman in the business...
I know that their hearts throbbed heavily and thumped a steady tempo with the big drum that was pounding out the rhythm as the flag slowly crawled up the centerfield mast.

And then there was a tremendous roar as the flag reached its crest and unfurled gloriously in the brilliant April sunlight ... The 25,000 fans settled back in their seats, ready for the ballgame as the Jersey City Giants jogged out to their positions ... Robinson was the second batter and as he strolled to the plate the crowd gave him an enthusiastic reception ... They were for him ... They all knew how he had overcome many obstacles in the deep South, how he had been barred from playing in Sanford, Fla., Jacksonville, Savannah and Richmond ... And yet, through it all, he was standing at the plate as the second baseman of the Montreal team ... The applause they gave so willingly was a salute of appreciation and admiration ... Robinson then socked a sizzler to the shortstop and was thrown out by an eyelash at first base.

The second time he appeared at the plate marked the beginning of what can develop into a great career. He got his first hit as a member of the Montreal Royals ... It was a mighty home run over the left field fence ... With two mates on the base paths, he walloped the first pitch that came his way and there was an explosive "crack" as bat and ball met ... The ball glistened brilliantly in the afternoon sun as it went hurtling high and far over the left field fence ... And, the white flag on the foul-line pole in left fluttered lazily as the ball whistled by.

HE GOT A GREAT OVATION FROM TEAM, FANS

Robinson jogged around the bases—his heart singing, a broad smile on his beaming bronze face as his two teammates trotted homeward ahead of him . . . When he rounded third, Manager Clay Hopper, who was coaching there, gave him a heavy pat on the back and shouted: "That's the way to hit that ball!" . . . Between third and home-plate he received another ovation from the stands, and then the entire Montreal team stood up and welcomed him to the bench . . . White hands slapping him on his broad back . . . Deep Southern voices from the bench shouted, "Yo sho' hit 'at one, Robbie, nice goin' kid!" . . . Another said: "Them folks 'at wouldn't let you play down in Jacksonville should be hee'ah now. Whoopee!" . . . And still another: "They cain't stop ya now, Jackie, you're really goin' places, and we're going to be right there with ya!" . . . Jackie Robinson laughed softly and smiled . . . Johnny Wright, wearing a big, blue pitcher's jacket, laughed and smiled . . . And, high up in the press box, Joe Bostic of the Amsterdam News and I looked at each other knowingly, and, we, too, laughed and smiled . . . Our hearts beat just a bit faster, and the thrill ran through us like champagne bubbles . . . It was a great day in Jersey . . . It was a great day in baseball!

But he didn't stop there, this whirlwind from California's gold coast . . . he ran the bases like a wild colt from the Western plains.

He laid down two perfect bunts and slashed a hit into rightfield...
He befuddled the pitchers, made them balk when he was roaring up
and down the base paths, and demoralized the entire Jersey
City team... He was a hitting demon and a base-running
maniac... The crowd gasped in amazement... The opposing
pitchers shook their heads in helpless agony... His understand-
ing teammates cheered him on with unrivaled enthusiasm...
And Branch Rickey, the man who had the fortitude and courage to sign him, heard the phenomenal news via telephone in
the offices of the Brooklyn Dodgers at Ebbets Field and said
admiringly—"He's a wonderful boy, that Jackie Robinson—a
wonderful boy!"

THEY MOBBED HIM AFTER THE GAME

When the game ended and Montreal had chalked up a 14 to 1
triumph, Robinson dashed for the club house and the showers...
But before he could get there he was surrounded by a howling
mob of kids, who came streaming out of the bleachers and
stands... They swept down upon him like a great ocean wave
and he was drowned in a sea of adolescent enthusiasm... There
he was—this Pied Piper of the diamond—perspiration rolling off
his bronze brow, idolizing kids swirling all around him, autograph
hounds tugging at him... And big cops riding prancing steeds
trying unsuccessfully to disperse the mob that had cornered the

70

hero of the day... One of his own teammates fought his way through the howling mob and finally "saved" Robinson... It was Red Durrett, who was a hero in his own right because he had pounded out two prodigious home runs himself, who came to the "rescue." He grabbed Robinson by the arm and pulled him through the crowd. "Come on," Durrett demanded, "you'll be here all night if you don't fight them off. They'll mob you. You can't possibly sign autographs for all those kids."

So, Jackie Robinson, escorted by the red-head outfielder, finally made his way to the dressing room. Bedlam broke loose in there, too... Photographers, reporters, kibitzers and hangers-on fenced him in... It was a virtual madhouse... His teammates, George Shuba, Stan Breard, Herman Franks, Tom Tatum, Marvin Rackley and all the others, were showering congratulations on him... They followed him into the showers, back to his locker and all over the dressing room... Flash bulbs flashed and reporters fired questions with machine-gun like rapidity... And Jackie Robinson smiled through it all.

As he left the park and walked out onto the street, the once-brilliant sun was fading slowly in the distant western skies... His petite and dainty little wife greeted him warmly and kindly. "You've had quite a day, little man," she said sweetly.

"Yes," he said softly and pleasantly, "God has been good to us today!"

THE ONLY WAY I'D WORRY ABOUT THE WEATHER IS IF IT SNOWS ON OUR SIDE OF THE FIELD AND NOT THEIRS.

—TOMMY LASORDA

Giants' Garlic Fries

San Francisco offers a great view of the ocean and plenty of delicious snacks during the game, including fantastic garlic fries. Our recipe doesn't require you to fry them, so they're as close to health food as baseball may ever get!

1. Preheat the oven to 450 degrees.

2. Combine all the ingredients in a bowl. Arrange on a baking sheet.

3. Bake 25 minutes or until brown. Serve with ketchup.

Serves 8.

3 pounds peeled baking potatoes, cut into strips

2 tablespoons vegetable oil

1/2 teaspoon each salt, garlic powder, paprika, and pepper

2 tablespoons grated Parmesan cheese

WHAT'S IN A NAME?
TEAM MONIKERS

☆ Originally the Pilgrims or the Puritans, the Red Socks got their name in 1901 when the new owner, John Taylor, thought they should have a name with more pizzazz and changed it to the Red Stockings. The sportswriters later shortened it.

☆ The sportswriter Phil Reed dubbed the Detroit Tigers the Tigers, because he thought their black and orange socks were reminiscent of Princeton University's Tigers.

☆ The Minnesota Twins were named for the nickname of their hometown—the "Twin Cities," Minneapolis and St. Paul.

☆ The Seattle Mariners were named in honor of the Pacific Northwest's nautical background

- Nothing invokes respect from an opposing team like the image of Texas's famous lawmen, the Rangers, whose name the Texas Rangers borrowed when they moved from Washington to to their new home in Arlington, Texas, in 1971.

- The Toronto Blue Jays were a brand new franchise when a fan contest was held to name them in 1977.

- Many clubs earned names from their owners affiliations or surname. The Atlanta Braves were first known as the Doves, after owner George Dovey, and then later, in 1912, as the Braves, a name inspired by new owner Jim Gaffney, a Tammany Hall chieftain.

- In 1901, two sportswriters in Chicago, Rice and Hayner, coined the name "Cubs" because the team was filled with an unusual amount of young players.

- The Cincinatti Reds were aptly named for the color of their socks. During the Cold War, however, that was temporarily changed to the Red Legs, since "Reds" was considered derogatory.

- Though briefly called the Bridegrooms after three players were married during the off-season, the Dodgers' name makes reference to the turn-of-the-century Brooklyn term, "Trolley Dodger."

- Based in the Great Metropolis, the name of the New York Mets is short for Metropolitans.

- In 1891, the Pittsburgh Pirates "stole" their cross-state rivals (the Phillies) best second-baseman, Lou Bierbauer, and thus earned the name of Pirates.

- Jim Mutrie, the 1895 manager of the team that would become the San Francisco Giants, endearingly referred to his players as "my giants" and the name stuck.

- Formerly known as the Colt 45s, the Houston Astros were renamed in 1965 in homage to Houston's new NASA Space Center.

SIXTY **FEET, SIX INCHES FROM HOME PLATE** is where it all begins in the game of baseball. The men who toe the rubber are surrounded by constant distractions—weather, base runners, umpires, coaches, and, most importantly, batters. The best

MEN ON THE MOUND

not only remain confident, but also have rhythm, balance, a variety of pitches, knowledge of each new batter, and incredible mental and physical toughness.

When talking about pitchers, it starts with the likes of Cy Young and Grover Cleveland Alexander, who worked the mound when it was only 50 feet from home plate. Alexander, a hard drinker from the Cardinals' lineup, suffered from epilepsy but still managed to win 373 games over 20 years. Cy Young, with a whopping 511 career victories, holds the throne for most wins in history. Young's durability and Alexander's sidearm throw are classic representations of dead-ball-area pitching.

At the turn of the 20th century, there was Christy Mathewson, a college-educated right-hander who played for the New York Giants from 1900 to 1916. Matty quickly earned the reputation for having the sharpest mind in the game. He could learn new pitches quickly and developed an arsenal of more than a dozen, which was uncommon at the time, including his trademark slider. He won 373 games, at least 22 per season for 12 seasons straight. His counterpart at the time was Walter "Big Train" Johnson of the Washington Senators.

Known for one pitch, his blazing fastball, he holds the record for the most shutouts ever: 110.

Lefty Grove, a pitcher for the Philadelphia A's during the '20s and '30s, did not share the likable and calm personas of Matty and Walter. He had a fiery temper and a fireball to match. Once striking out Babe Ruth three times and Lou Gehrig twice in one game, Grove led his team to the World Series three years in a row. Near the end of Lefty's career, a 17-year-old upstart's pitches were clocked at 98 miles an hour. "Rapid Robert," or Bob Feller, was poised to replace Lefty as baseball's next great pitcher. Feller joined the Cleveland Indians in 1936 and spent 18 years on the mound smoking his opponents.

In the years that followed, great pitchers seemed hard to find. Then came Warren Spahn. Spahn, who had earned a Purple Heart and Bronze Star in World War II, reminded America that pitchers could be as legendary as home-run hitters. Signed by the Braves in 1942, he was praised for his style on the mound, and over his 21-year career became the winningest southpaw in history.

Continuing Spahn's standard of excellence were two pitchers who began their careers in the mid-'50s, Sandy Koufax and Bob Gibson. It took Koufax six years to become a superstar pitcher in the majors. When he learned to handle the pressure, Sandy drew 10,000 to 20,000 fans to Dodgers games with his hopping fastball and devastating curve. Gibson, a former Harlem Globetrotter, was the big-game Cardinal pitcher for more than 17 years. In his career, he pitched three no-hitters in a single World Series, twice. A true competitor, Gibson was left in a World Series game after nine straight innings because his manager, Johnny Keane, believed in his heart.

The next pitcher in line to capture America's imagination was Nolan Ryan. He, like Koufax, came into his own slowly before being traded to the California Angels in 1972. After four years in the majors, Ryan's work ethic began to pay off, with his fastball clocking in at 100 miles per hour. Pitching through painful injuries, he played for an amazing 27 years. His long career was highlighted with 5,714 strikeouts and seven no-hitters, the last pitched when he was 44 years old.

These men have blazed the way for new legends, all trying to live up the pressures and the potential that the position offers. The talent is out there: Greg Maddux, Randy Johnson, Pedro Martinez, and Roger Clemens are just a few of the hurlers who are keeping the thinking man's game alive. For fans, watching each duel between the mound and the plate continues to thrill because pitch after pitch is full of strategy, skill, and a pitcher's iron will to better his last throw.

YOU SEE, YOU SPEND
A GOOD PIECE OF
YOUR LIFE GRIPPING
A BASEBALL, AND IN
THE END IT TURNS
OUT THAT IT WAS THE
OTHER WAY AROUND
ALL THE TIME.

—JIM BOUTON

83

GOD'S COUNTRY
AND MINE

BY JACQUES BARZUN

People who care less for gentility manage things better. They don't bother to leave the arid city but spend their surplus there on pastimes they can enjoy without feeling cramped. They follow boxing and wrestling, burlesque and vaudeville (when available), professional football and hockey. Above all, they thrill in unison with their fellow man the country over by watching baseball. The gods decree a heavyweight match only once in a while and a national election only every four years, but there is a World Series with every revolution of the earth around the sun. And in between, what varied pleasure long drawn out!

Whoever wants to know the heart and mind of America had better learn baseball, the rules and realities of the game—and do it by watching first some high school or small-town teams. The big league games are too fast for the beginner and the newspapers don't help. To read them with profit you have to know a language that comes easy only after philosophy has taught you to judge practice. Here is scholarship that takes effort on the part of the outsider, but it is so bred into the native that it never becomes

85

a dreary round of technicalities. The wonderful purging of the passions that we all experienced in the fall of '51, the despair groaned out over the fate of the Dodgers, from whom the league pennant was snatched at the last minute, give us some idea of what Greek tragedy was like. Baseball *is* Greek in being national, heroic, and broken up in the rivalries of city-states. How sad that Europe knows nothing like it! Its Olympics generate anger, not unity, and its interstate politics follow no rules that a people can grasp. At least Americans understand baseball, the true realm of clear ideas.

That baseball fitly expresses the powers of the nation's mind and body is a merit separate from the glory of being the most active, agile, varied, articulate, and brainy of all group games. It is of and for our century. Tennis belongs to the individualistic past—a hero, or at most a pair of friends or lovers, against the world. The idea of baseball is a team, an outfit, a section, a gang, a union, a cell, a commando squad—in short, a twentieth-century setup of opposite numbers.

Baseball takes its mystic nine and scatters them wide. A kind of individualism thereby returns, but it is limited—eternal vigilance is the price of victory. Just because they're far apart, the outfield can't dream or play she-loves-me-not with daisies. The infield is like a steel net held in the hands of the catcher. He is the psychologist and historian for the staff—or else his signals will give the opposition hits. The value of his headpiece is shown by the iron-mongery worn to protect it. The pitcher, on the other hand, is the wayward man of genius, whom others will direct. They will expect nothing from him but virtuosity. He is surrounded no doubt by mere talent, unless one excepts that transplanted acrobat, the shortstop. What a brilliant invention is his role despite its exposure to ludicrous lapses! One man to each base, and then the free lance, the trouble shooter, the movable feast for the eyes, whose motion animates the whole foreground.

The rules keep pace with this imaginative creation so rich in allusions to real life. How excellent, for instance, that a foul tip muffed by the catcher gives the batter another chance. It is the recognition of Chance that knows no argument. But on the other hand, how wise and just that the third strike must not be dropped. This points to the fact that near the end of any struggle life asks for more than is needful in order to clinch success. A victory has to be won, not snatched. We find also our American innocence in calling "World Series" the annual games between the winners in each big league. The world doesn't know or care and couldn't compete if it wanted to, but since it's us children having fun, why, the world is our stage. I said baseball was Greek. Is there not a poetic symbol in the new meaning—our meaning—of "Ruth hits Homer"?

Once the crack of the bat has sent the ball skimming left of second between the infielder's legs, six men converge or distend their defense to keep the runner from advancing along the prescribed path. The ball is not the center of interest as in those vulgar predatory games like football, basketball, and polo. Man running is the force to be contained. His getting to first or second base starts a capitalization dreadful to think of: every hit pushes him on. Bases full and a homer make four runs, while the defenders, helpless without the magic power of the ball lying over the fence, cry out their anguish and dig up the sod with their spikes.

But fate is controlled by the rules. Opportunity swings from one side to the other because innings alternate quickly, keep up spirit in the players, interest in the beholders. So does the profusion of different acts to be performed—pitching, throwing, catching, batting, running, stealing, sliding, signaling. Blows are similarly varied. Flies, Texas Leaguers, grounders, baseline fouls—praise God the human neck is a universal joint! And there is no set pace. Under the hot sun, the minutes creep as a deliberate pitcher tries his feints and curves for three strikes called, or conversely walks a threatening batter. But the batter is not invariably a tailor's dummy. In a hundredth of a second there may be a hissing rocket down right field, a cloud of dust over first base—the bleachers all a-yell—a double play and the other side up to bat.

Accuracy and speed, the practiced eye and hefty arm, the mind to take in and readjust to the unexpected, the possession of more than one talent and the willingness to work in harness without special orders—these are the American virtues that shine in baseball. There has never been a good player who was dumb. Beef and bulk and mere endurance count for little, judgment and daring for much. Baseball is among group games played with a ball what fencing is to games of combat. But being spread out, baseball has something sociable and friendly about it that I especially love. It is graphic and choreographic. The ball is not shuttling in a confined space, as in tennis. Nor does baseball go to the other extreme of solitary whanging and counting stopped on the brink of pointlessness, like golf. Baseball is a kind of collective chess with arms and legs in full play under sunlight.

How adaptable, too! Three kids in a back yard are enough to create the same quality of drama. All of us in our tennis days have pounded balls with a racket against a wall, for practice. But that is nothing compared with batting in an empty lot, or catching at twilight, with a fella who'll let you use his mitt when your palms get too raw. Every part of baseball equipment is inherently attractive and of a most enchanting functionalism. A man cannot have too much leather about him; and a catcher's mitt is just the right amount for one hand. It's too bad the chest protector and shinpads are so hot and at a distance so like corrugated cardboard. Otherwise, the team is elegance itself in its stripped knee breeches and loose shirts, colored stockings and peaked caps. Except for brief moments of sliding, you can see them all in one eyeful, unlike the muddy hecatombs of football. To watch a football game is to be in prolonged neurotic doubt as to what you're seeing. It's more like an emergency happening at a distance than a game. I don't wonder the spectators take to drink. Who has ever seen a baseball fan drinking within the meaning of the act? He wants all his senses sharp and clear, his eyesight above all. He gulps down soda pop, which is a harmless way of replenishing his energy by the ingestion of sugar diluted in water and colored pink.

Happy the man in the bleachers. He is enjoying the spectacle that the gods on Olympus contrived only with difficulty when they sent Helen to Troy and picked their teams. And the gods missed the fun of doing this by catching a bat near the narrow end and measuring hand over hand for first pick. In Troy, New York, the game scheduled for 2 P.M. will break no bones, yet it will be a real fight between Southpaw Dick and Red Larsen. For those whom civilized play doesn't fully satisfy, there will be provided a scapegoat in a blue suit—the umpire, yell-proof and even-handed as justice, which he demonstrates with outstretched arms when calling "Safe!"

And the next day in the paper: learned comment, statistical summaries, and the verbal imagery of meta-euphoric experts. In the face of so much joy, one can only ask, Were you there when Dogface Joe parked the pellet beyond the pale?

EVENING HOWLER
SPORTING EXTRA
"SLATS" KELLY'S THREE BAGGER
WINS IN THE TWELFTH

I'D RATHER SWING A BAT THAN DO ANYTHING ELSE IN THE WORLD.

—TED WILLIAMS

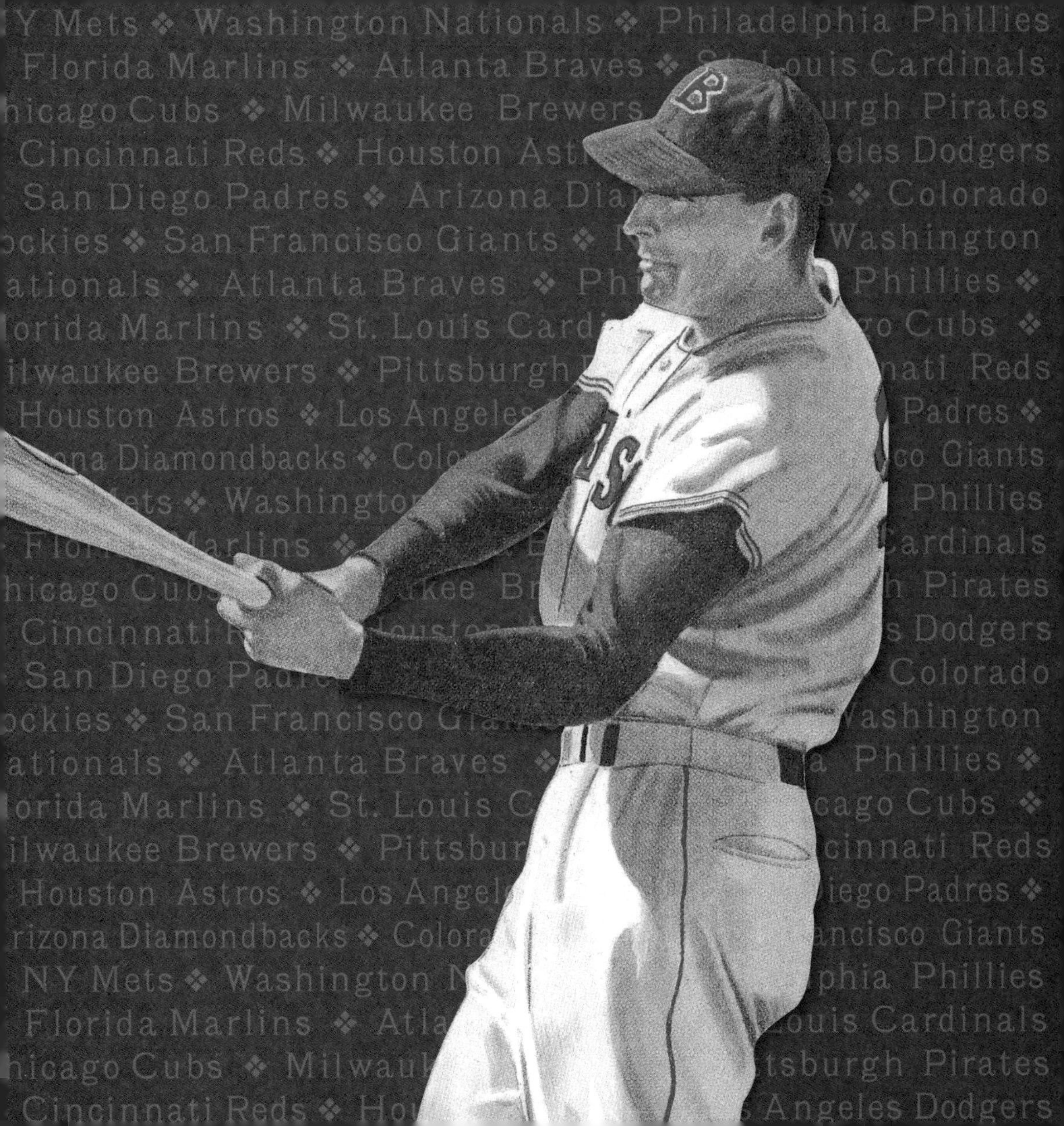
Y Mets ❖ Washington Nationals ❖ Philadelphia Phillies
Florida Marlins ❖ Atlanta Braves ❖ St. Louis Cardinals
hicago Cubs ❖ Milwaukee Brewers
urgh Pirates
Cincinnati Reds ❖ Houston Ast
eles Dodgers
San Diego Padres ❖ Arizona Dia
s ❖ Colorado
ockies ❖ San Francisco Giants ❖
Washington
ationals ❖ Atlanta Braves ❖ Ph
Phillies ❖
orida Marlins ❖ St. Louis Cardi
go Cubs ❖
ilwaukee Brewers ❖ Pittsburgh
nati Reds
Houston Astros ❖ Los Angeles
Padres ❖
ona Diamondbacks ❖ Colo
co Giants
Mets ❖ Washington
Phillies
Cardinals
hicago Cub
ukee
Pirates
Cincinnati
s Dodgers
San Diego Padre
Colorado
ockies ❖ San Francisco
Washington
ationals ❖ Atlanta Braves ❖
a Phillies ❖
orida Marlins ❖ St. Louis C
cago Cubs ❖
ilwaukee Brewers ❖ Pittsbur
cinnati Reds
Houston Astros ❖ Los Angel
Diego Padres ❖
rizona Diamondbacks ❖ Colora
ancisco Giants
NY Mets ❖ Washington N
phia Phillies
Florida Marlins ❖ Atla
Louis Cardinals
hicago Cubs ❖ Milwauk
tsburgh Pirates
Cincinnati Reds ❖ Ho
s Angeles Dodgers

Ted Williams's Hall of Fame Acceptance Speech

July 25, 1966, Cooperstown, N.Y.

Ballplayers are not born great. They're not born great hitters or pitchers or managers, and luck isn't a big factor. No one has come up for a substitute for hard work. I've never met a great baseball player who didn't have to work harder at learning to play ball than anything else he ever did. To me it was the greatest fun I ever had, which probably explains why today I feel both humility and pride, because God let me play the game and learn to be good at it. Proud because I spent most of my life in the company of so many wonderful people. There are plaques dedicated to baseball men of all generations and I am privileged to join them.

Baseball gives every American boy a chance to excel, not just to be as good as someone else, but to be better than someone else. This is the nature of man and the name of the game and I have always been a very lucky guy to wear a baseball uniform, to have struck out or hit, or take a major Home Run. I hope that some day the names of Satchel Paige and Josh Gibson in some way could be added as a symbol of the great Negro players that are not here only because they were not given the chance. And I know Casey Stengel feels the same way, and I'm awfully glad to be with him on his big day. I also know I'll lose a dear friend if I don't stop talking, because I know that I'm eating into his time, and that is unforgivable. So in closing, I am grateful and know how lucky I was to have been born an American and to have had the chance to play the game I love, the greatest game of them all baseball.

Doubleday Field in Cooperstown, New York, where the National Hall of Fame game is played every summer.

In 1905, the Mills Commission was created to determine the true origins of baseball. Thanks largely to the testimony of Abner Graves, the commission determined that Major General Abner Doubleday modified a game of town ball into the current idea of baseball while he was at school in Cooperstown, New York.

When an old baseball was discovered in 1934 in a farmhouse a few miles from Cooperstown, resident Stephen C. Clark decided to put the "Doubleday Baseball" on display along with other baseball objects. With the backing of Alexander Cleveland and the baseball commissioner, the National Baseball Museum and Hall of Fame was opened in 1939.

The U.S. postmaster general released a commemorative baseball stamp on June 12, 1939, the same day that the museum was officially dedicated.

The first Hall of Fame election took place in 1936. The first five players inducted were Ty Cobb, Babe Ruth, Honus Wagner, Christy Mathewson, and Walter Johnson.

COOPERSTOWN, NEW YORK

- Long after Cooperstown was declared the birthplace of baseball, doubts persisted. In 1999, papers of the commission were found, leading to the now commonly held belief that baseball was invented much earlier, possibly even the late 1700s—though exactly when cannot be proven.

- More than 350,000 people travel to Cooperstown to visit the museum each year.

- The museum has more than 35,000 three-dimensional artifacts—including bats, balls, and uniforms—and 130,000 baseball cards.

- The Hall of Fame library has 2.6 million items, with more than 10,000 hours of film and sound footage.

- Aside from artifacts, the museum hosts a large collection of artworks related to baseball and the interactive Sandlot Kids' Clubhouse.

- To be eligible for the Hall of Fame, a player must have retired five years prior and have played in each of 10 championship seasons. Players who have passed away can be considered for election within 6 months.

- Hall of Famers voters must have been active or honorary members of the Baseball Writers' Association of America for 10 years. They can vote for up to 10 eligible players, and any candidate who receives 75 percent of the vote is inducted.

- Every year an interleague game is played by two major-league teams in Cooperstown during Induction Weekend. The first Hall of Fame Game, played in 1940, featured the Cubs and Red Sox.

- No Hall of Famer has ever been inducted with 100 percent of the possible votes.

- Jackie Robinson was the first black ballplayer inducted into the Hall of Fame, in 1962.

- Shoeless Joe Jackson is not in the Hall of Fame, because any player who is on baseball's ineligible list cannot be inducted.

- The museum once featured an exhibit called "You're in the Hall of Fame Now, Charlie Brown", which celebrated baseball strips from the comic strip *Peanuts*.

St. Louis Cardinals' Outta the Park Nachos

Celebrate an old World Series winner with these Busch Stadium favorites. The 1942 World Champion Cardinals were nicknamed "the St. Louis Swifties" for their outstanding hustle—something you'll need, too, if you want to get any of these tasty nachos before they're history.

1. Preheat the oven to 400 degrees.

2. In a saucepan, mix the refried beans and taco seasoning. Cook over medium heat until bubbly. Remove from the heat.

3. In a small bowl, combine the tomatoes and cilantro until well blended.

4. In a separate bowl, mash the avocados with the lemon juice until well blended.

5. Arrange the chips evenly on a large cookie sheet or oven-proof platter. Spread a layer of refried beans on the chips. Sprinkle the cheese over the beans; spread the tomatoes on top. Bake 3 to 5 minutes, or until the cheese has melted.

6. Spoon the avocado mixture on top of the nachos. Top with sour cream. Sprinkle with sliced chilies if desired. Eat immediately!

Serves 8 to 10.

---

1 16-ounce can refried beans

1 tablespoon taco seasoning

2 cups tomatoes, diced

2 tablespoons cilantro, minced

2 avocados

2 teaspoons lemon juice

1 8- to 10-ounce bag tortilla chips

1/4 pound grated Monterey Jack cheese

1/4 pound grated cheddar cheese

8 ounces sour cream

3 jalapeño peppers, minced (optional)

Line-up for Yesterday

An ABC of Baseball Immortals

Ogden Nash

A is for Alex
The great Alexander;
More goose eggs he pitched
Than a popular gander.

B is for Bresnahan
Back of the plate;
The Cubs were his love,
And McGraw his hate.

C is for Cobb,
Who grew spikes and not corn,
And made all the basemen
Wish they weren't born.

D is for Dean,
The grammatical Diz,
When the asked, Who's the tops?
Said correctly, I is.

E is for Evers,
His jaw in advance;
Never afraid
To Tinker with Chance.

F is for Fordham
And Frankie and Frisch;
I wish he were back
With the Giants, I wish.

G is for Gehrig,
The Pride of the Stadium;
His record pure gold,
His courage, pure radium.

H is for Hornsby;
When pitching to Rog,
The pitcher would pitch,
Then the pitcher would dodge.

103

I is for Me,
Not a hard-hitting man,
But an outstanding all-time
Incurable fan.

J is for Johnson
The Big Train in his prime
Was so fast he could throw
Three strikes at a time.

K is for Keeler,
As fresh as green paint,
The fastest and mostest
To hit where they ain't.

L is Lajoie
Whom Clevelanders love,
Napoleon himself,
With glue in his glove.

M is for Matty,
Who carried a charm
In the form of an extra
Brain in his arm.

N is for Newsom,
Bobo's favorite kin.
You ask how he's here,
He talked himself in.

O is for Ott
Of the restless right foot.
When he leaned on the pellet,
The pellet stayed put.

P is for Plank,
The arm of the A's;
When he tangled with Matty
Games lasted for days.

Q is Don Quixote
Cornelius Mack;
Neither Yankees nor years
Can halt his attack.

R is for Ruth.
To tell you the truth,
There's no more to be said,
Just R is for Ruth.

S is for Speaker,
Swift center-field tender,
When the ball saw him coming,
It yelled, "I surrender."

T is for Terry
The Giant from Memphis
Whose .400 average
You can't overemphis.

U would be 'Ubbell
If Carl were a cockney;
We say Hubbell and baseball
Like football and Rockne.

V is for Vance
The Dodger's own Dazzy;
None of his rivals
Could throw as fast as he.

W, Wagner,
The bowlegged beauty;
Short was closed to all traffic
With Honus on duty.

X is the first
Of two x's in Foxx
Who was right behind Ruth
With his powerful soxx.

Y is for Young
The magnificent Cy;
People battled against him,
But I never knew why.

Z is for Zenith
The summit of fame.
These men are up there.
These men are the game.

I DON'T WANT TO PLAY GOLF. WHEN I HIT A BALL, I WANT SOMEBODY ELSE TO GO CHASE IT.

—ROGERS HORNSBY

LOUISVILLE SLUGGER

BY BOB GREENE

At the newspaper where I work we have a rule that staff members are not allowed to accept any gift of significant value from an outside source. The rule probably makes sense; its purpose is to prevent potential news sources from trying to influence news coverage through the bestowing of lavish presents.

But I recently received something in the mail from an outside company, and if the newspaper makes me give it back they're going to have to drag me out of here kicking and screaming and holding on to it for dear life.

The package was long and narrow. I opened it. Inside was something that brought tears to my eyes and a funny feeling to my throat:

A Louisville Slugger baseball bat—a Bob Greene autographed model.

For five minutes I sat there looking at it and caressing it and speaking softly to it.

There, in the middle of the barrel, was the Louisville Slugger logo, and the famous copyrighted slogan: "Powerized." There, next to the logo, was the trademark of the Hillerich & Bradsby Co., which manufactures Louisville Sluggers.

And there—right at the end of the barrel—were the words PERSONAL MODEL—LOUISVILLE SLUGGER. And where Mickey Mantle's or Hank Aaron's autograph ought to be, the script words "Bob Greene."

I suppose there must be some item that an American boy might treasure more fiercely than a Louisville Slugger with his own signature on it, but I can't think of one. For all of us who grew up on sandlots and playgrounds, gripping Louisville Sluggers bearing the autographs of major league stars, the thought of owning one with our own name on the barrel is almost too much to comprehend.

In the box with the Louisville Slugger was a letter from John A. Hillerich III, president of Hillerich & Bradsby. In the letter Hillerich said that this is the centennial year for Louisville Sluggers; the first one was manufactured in the spring of 1884. Thus, the enclosed bat—a memento of the 100th anniversary.

When I started to show my new bat to people, the response I got was interesting. Women seemed not to care too much; generally they said something like, "Oh, a baseball bat." They would inspect it a little more closely, and then say, "What's your name doing on it?"

But men—men were a different story. First they would see the bat.

They'd say something like, "A real Louisville Slugger. That's great." Invariably they would lift it up and go into a batting stance—perhaps for the first time in twenty or thirty years. Then they would roll the bat around in their hands—and finally they would see the signature.

That's when they'd get faint in the head. They would look as if they were about to swoon. Their eyes would start to resemble pinwheels. And in reverential whispers, they would say: "That is the most wonderful thing I have ever seen. Your own name on a Louisville Slugger. You are so lucky."

For it is true: a Louisville Slugger, for the American male, is a talisman—a piece of property that carries such symbolic weight and meaning that words of description do not do it justice. I have a friend who has two photographs mounted above his desk at work. One photo shows Elvis Presley kissing a woman. The other shows Ted Williams kissing his Louisville Slugger. No one ever asks my friend the meaning of those pictures; the meaning, of course, is quite clear without any explanation.

Hillerich & Bradsby has a photo in its archives that is similarly moving. In the photo, Babe Ruth and Lou Gehrig are standing in a batting cage. Gehrig, a wide smile on his face, is examining the bat. Perhaps you could find another photo that contains three figures more holy to the American male than those three—Ruth, Gehrig, and a Louisville Slugger—but I don't know where you'd look.

Hillerich & Bradsby has some intriguing figures and facts about Louisville Sluggers. The company manufactures approximately one million of them each year. That requires the use of about two hundred thousand trees each baseball season; the company owns five thousand acres of timberland in Pennsylvania and New York to provide the trees. Ash timber is the wood of choice for Louisville Sluggers. Years ago, the wood of choice was hickory.

According to the company, a professional baseball player uses an average of seventy-two bats each season—which comes as a surprise to those of us who always envisioned a major leaguer using the same special good-luck bat for years on end. The company says that, during World War II, some American sporting goods found their way to a German prison camp in Upper Silesia; the American prisoners of war there reportedly cried at the sight of the Louisville Sluggers. During the Korean War, an American soldier reportedly dashed out of his trench during a firefight to retrieve a Louisville Slugger he had left out in the open before the battle began.

❖ ❖ ❖

As I sit here typing this, a colleague—a male—has just walked up next to my computer terminal, lifted my Louisville Slugger to his shoulder, and gone into a batter's crouch. In a moment, if I'm right, he'll start examining the bat—and in another moment he'll see the autograph.

I can't wait.

Hurrah for Our National Game

BY WALTER NEVILLE

Hurrah for our game, our National game
There's health in its ev'ry bound.
A thrill of delight in its very name
A joy in its simplest sound;

It lends new strength to our hardy race,
And its pleasures are never tame,
Then here's to the bat, the ball, and the base,
Hurrah for our National Game.

Then hurrah for our National Game, hurrah,
Here's a cheer for its well-earned fame,
Success to it ever, Hurrah, hurrah,
Hurrah for our National Game.

The timid lament ov'r such dangerous fun,
And groan at "that terrible ball,"
The lazy ones shrink from making "a run"
And cowards are fearing a fall;

But give us the dash of a strong "home strike"
And we laugh such folly to shame:
Take all other sports and do what you like
But leave us our National Game.

Then hurrah for our National Game, hurrah,
Here's a cheer for its well-earned fame,
Success to it ever, Hurrah, hurrah,
Hurrah for our National Game.

The Gamester may boast of the pleasures of play,
The Billiardist brag of his cue.
The Horse-Jockey gabble of next racing day.
The Yachtman discourse of the Blue.

The patrons of Racket may feast on its joys,
Whilst Cricket its lovers inflames,
Croquet's very well for young ladies and boys
But give us the National Game.

Then hurrah for our National Game, hurrah,
Here's a cheer for its well-earned fame,
Success to it ever, Hurrah, hurrah,
Hurrah for our National Game.

Now toss for the innings, the bases are down
Outsiders go to the field,
The scorer with tallies successes will crown,
As each striker "the willow" doth wield.

The Captains assign each player his place,
The Umpire his rulings will name,
To all their decisions submit with good grace
As required by our National Game.

Then hurrah for our National Game, hurrah,
Here's a cheer for its well-earned fame,
Success to it ever, Hurrah, hurrah,
Hurrah for our National Game.

And thus 'tis in life, each one has a post,
Assigned by the Captain of all,
While the great Umpire "Conscience" is guiding the host
Take heed that we list to his call.

May no "base play" be ours, may our record be bright
With no foul deeds our "clean score" to shame
Let us play life's game nobly, respecting the right
As we do in our National Game.

Then hurrah for our National Game, hurrah,
Here's a cheer for its well-earned fame,
Success to it ever, Hurrah, hurrah,
Hurrah for our National Game.

Hurrah.

LISTEN UP:
BASEBALL SONGS & SOUNDS

☆ During the seventh-inning stretch in Game 1 of the 1918 World Series, a military band played "The Star Spangled Banner" as a tribute to all servicemen on leave and in attendance. From then on, the song was played at every World Series outing and every season opener (though it was not yet the national anthem). It wasn't until the '40s that the custom of playing it before every game began, thanks to the installation of stadium speakers.

☆ Cincinnati Reds announcer Harry Hartman was the first to use the phrase "Going, going, gone!" to describe a home run, in the '30s.

☆ Baseball announcer Harry Caray always led Cubs fans in a seventh-inning-stretch rendition of "Take Me Out to the Ballgame," and it became a beloved tradition at Wrigley Field.

☆ In 1997, the Toronto Blue Jays hosted the Montreal Expos in an all-Canadian affair as part of the new interleague schedule, marking the first time since World War II that the U.S. national anthem was not heard before a major-league ball game.

- The first baseball game was broadcast on the radio by Harold Alren from KDKA in Pittsburgh on August 25, 1921.

- In the '20s, most radio announcers received telegraph messages while the team was playing an away game, and the announcers would re-create the game, play by play, from the incoming messages.

- It wasn't until 1935 that a team owner allowed every season game to be broadcast for radio listeners. That owner was William Wrigley of the Chicago Cubs.

- During World War II, the Office of Censorship banned announcers from any mention of weather conditions during their baseball broadcasts for fear that enemies wanting to attack the city would receive valuable information.

- The National Baseball Museum and Hall of Fame honors the best announcers of the game with the Ford C. Frick Award every year at the induction ceremony. The first award was given in 1978 to two of the game's most beloved voices, Mel Allen and Red Barber.

- Ronald Reagan—before becoming president and even before his acting career began—was a baseball announcer, translating telegraphs into games for his listeners.

- Many announcers have created their own unique way of calling a home run, including Jack Brickhouse's "Whoo hoo, boy! Next time around, bring me back my stomach!" Vin Scully's "Forget it!" Jerry Trupiano's "... swing and there it goes... light tower power!" and, most memorably, Rosey Roswell's "Open the window, Aunt Minnie, here it comes!"

- Jack Norworth and Albert Von Tilzer, composers of "Take Me Out to the Ball Game," had never seen a baseball game when they wrote the now famous anthem in 1908. In fact, it wasn't until 20 years after the song was written that Von Tilzer finally saw his first game. His partner, Norworth, didn't reach the inside of a stadium until 1949, when the Brooklyn Dodgers honored him at Ebbets Field.

THIS IS LIKE DÉJÀ VÙ ALL OVER AGAIN.
—YOGI BERRA

121

A MATTER OF RECORD

BY GEORGE PLIMPTON

It was a simple act by an unassuming man which touched an enormous circle of people, indeed an entire country. It provided an instant which people would remember for decades—exactly what they were doing at the time of the home run that beat Babe Ruth's great record of 714 home runs which had stood for 39 years, whether they were watching it on a television set, or heard it over the car radio while driving along the turnpike at night, or whether a neighbor leaned over a picket fence and told them about it the next morning.

Its effect was far-reaching, and more powerful than one would expect from the act of hitting a ball over a fence. The Mexico sports correspondent from *El Sol de Mexico*, almost overcome with emotion, ended his piece on the Aaron 715th home run with thanks to God. "We lived through this historic moment, the most fabulous in the world. Thanks to God we witnessed this moment of history."

In Japan the huge headlines in Tokyo's premier sports daily read haikulike: WHITE BALL DANCES THROUGH ATLANTA'S WHITE MIST

and under the subhead I Saw It the correspondent began: "In my Atlanta hotel room I now begin writing this copy. I know I have to be calm. But I find it impossible to prevent my writing hand from continuing to shake..."

It caused tragedy. In Jacksonville, Florida, a taxicab driver shot himself when his wife pulled him out of his chair in front of the television to send him out to work just as he was settling down to the game. He died before the home run was hit....

Almost everyone in baseball was in front of a television set. In Kansas City the ancient black pitcher Satchel Paige had seventeen of his family crowded around ("all these sisters-in-law of mine") and when they saw the ball hit they began shouting and they could hear the people next door carrying on the same way.

For those who sat in the stadium in Atlanta their recollections would be especially intimate—the sharp cork-pop sound of the bat hitting the ball, startlingly audible in that split second of suspense before the crowd began a roar that lasted for more than ten minutes. Perhaps that is what they would remember—how people stood in front of their seats and sucked in air and bellowed it out in a sustained tribute that no other athlete has ever received. Or perhaps they would remember the wonder at how easy and inevitable it seemed—that having opened the season in Cincinnati by hitting the tying home run number 714 with his first swing of the year, it was obviously appropriate that the man called "Supe" by his teammates (for Superman) was going to duplicate the feat in Atlanta with his first swing of *that* game to break the record. That was why 53,775 had come. Or perhaps they would remember the odd way the stadium emptied after the excitement of the fourth inning, as if the crowd felt that what they had seen would be diluted by sitting through any more baseball that night.

But finally there were those few in the core of that immense circle—the participants themselves—who would be the ones most keenly touched: the pitcher, in this case a gap-toothed pleasant veteran named Al Downing who of the more than one hundred National League pitchers happened to be the one who threw a fast ball at a certain moment that did not tail away properly; the hitter, Henry Aaron himself, for whom the event, despite his grace in dealing with it, had become so traumatic that little in the instant was to be relished except the relief that it had been done; the Braves' sports announcer, whose imagination for months had been working up words to describe the event to the outside world; and a young bullpen pitcher who would reach in the air and establish contact with a ball whose value as baseball's greatest talisman had been monetarily pegged at $25,000 and whose sentimental value was incalculable....

THE HITTER

On occasion, as Henry Aaron sits in the Braves' dugout, he takes off his baseball cap and holds it close against his face. He moves it around until he is able to peer through one of the ventholes in the crown of the cap at the opposing pitcher on the mound. The practice, like focusing through a telescope, serves to isolate the pitcher, setting him apart in a round frame so that Aaron can scrutinize him and decide how he will deal with him once he reaches the plate.

The thought process he goes through during this is to decide what sort of pitch during his stand at the plate he will almost surely see... engraving this possibility in his mind's eye so that when the pitch comes (almost as if dictating what he wants) he can truly rip at it. Home-run hitters must invariably be "guessers," since their craft depends on seeing a pitch come down that they *expect*—so they have time to generate a powerful swing. More than one pitcher had said that Aaron seems to hop on a pitch as if he had called for it. Ron Perranoski, an ex-Dodger relief pitcher who in his first six seasons against Aaron held him to an .812 average (13 for 16), once said: "He not only knows what the pitch will be, but *where* it will be."

Aaron describes his mental preparation as a process of elimination. "Suppose a pitcher has three good pitches—a fast ball, a curve, and a slider. What I do, after a lot of consideration and analyzing and studying, is to eliminate two of those pitches, since it's impossible against a good pitcher to keep all three possibilities on my mind at the plate. So in getting rid of two, for example, I convince myself that I'm going to get a fast ball down low. When it comes, I'm ready. Now I can have guessed *wrong*, and if I've set my mind for a fast ball it's hard to do much with a curve, short of nibbling it out over the infield. But the chances are that I'll eventually get what I'm looking for."

The procedure of "guessing" has many variants. Roger Maris, for one, went up to the plate always self-prepared to hit a fast ball, feeling that he was quick enough to adjust to a different sort of pitch as it flew toward the plate. Most "guess" hitters play a cat-and-mouse game with the pitcher as the count progresses. What distinguishes Aaron's system is that once he makes up his mind what he will see during a time at bat he never deviates. He has disciplined himself to sit and wait for one sort of pitch whatever the situation.

One might suppose that a pitcher with a large repertoire of stuff would trouble Aaron—and that indeed turns out to be the case. He shakes his head when he thinks of Juan Marichal. "When he's at the prime of his game he throws a good fast ball, a good screwball, a good change-up, a good slider, a good you-have-it . . .

and obviously the elimination system can't work; you can't throw out five or six different pitches in the hope of seeing one; the odds of seeing it would be too much against the batter."

What to do against a Marichal then? "It's an extra challenge," Aaron says. "I've just got to tune up my bat a little higher. It's a question of confidence, *knowing* that the pitcher cannot get me out four times without me hitting the ball sharply somewhere."

It is this confrontation between pitcher and hitter that fascinates Aaron, and indeed it is what he likes best about baseball— what he called "that damn good guessing game."

"So much of it has to do with concentration," Aaron explained to me. "On the day of a night game I begin concentrating at four in the afternoon. Just before I go to bat, from the on-deck circle, I can hear my little girl—she's 12 now—calling from the stands, 'Hey daddy! Hey, daddy!' After the game she says to me, 'Hey, you never look around, daddy, to wave.' Well, sometimes I look at her, I can't help it, but not too often. I'm looking at the pitcher. I'm thinking very hard about him."

His discipline is so extreme that not only does Aaron not hear anything when he gets to the plate, simply sealed in his vacuum of concentration, but his habits are so strictly adhered to that over the years he has never seen one of his home runs land in the stands. He is too busy getting down the first-base line.

I said I couldn't believe him. I must have sounded petulant about it because his brown eyes looked at me quickly.

"What I mean is," I said, "that I can't imagine denying oneself the pleasure of seeing the results of something like that. I mean it's like finishing a painting with one grand stroke of the brush and not stepping back to look at it."

I knew that most players do watch the home runs drop, at least the long ones, dawdling just out of the batter's box on that slow trot, the head turned. In the films of Bobby Thomson's Miracle home run in 1951 against the Dodgers in the playoffs at the Polo Grounds, it is quite apparent, his face in profile, that he glories in the drive going in; in fact, he does a small hop of delight halfway down the first-base line.

"Well, that's not what I'm supposed to do," Aaron was saying. "I've seen guys miss first base looking to see where the ball went. My job is to get down to first base and touch it. Looking at the ball going over the fence isn't going to help. I don't even look at the home runs in batting practice. No sense to break a good habit."

The odd thing about Aaron's attitude at the plate is that there is nothing to suggest any such intensity of purpose. His approach is slow and lackadaisical. He was called "Snowshoes" for a time by his teammates for the way he sort of pushes himself along. He carries his batting helmet on his way, holding two bats in the

129

other hand. He stares out at the pitcher. He drops the extra bat. Then, just out of the batting box, resting his bat on the ground with the handle end balanced against his thighs, he uses both hands to jostle the helmet correctly into position. He steps into the box. Even here there is no indication of the kinetic possibility—none of the ferocious tamping of his spikes to get a good toehold that one remembers of Willie Mays, say, and the quick switching of his bat back and forth as he waits. Aaron steps into the batter's box as if he were gong to sit down in it somewhere. His attitude is such that Robin Roberts, the Phillies pitcher, once explained, "That's why you can't fool Aaron. He falls asleep between pitches."

Jim Brosnan, ex-pitcher and author of the fine baseball chronicle *The Long Season*, once told me, "It was odd pitching to him. I always had a lot of confidence—perhaps because he walked up the way he did and because he stood so far away from the plate, just as far away as he could. That made you think that he wasn't fearless, which is good for a pitcher's morale. It looked as though he was giving away the outside of the plate to the pitcher, like he didn't want to stand in there and protect it. Still, I gave up two home runs to him. Funny, I don't remember one of them at all. I must have made a mistake, which I have made so many of that I tend to forget. But the other I remember because it was made off a perfect pitch, right in that classic spot where you're supposed to pitch to him, and he reached over, and those wrists of his snapped, and it was gone. I was so startled that I thought I'd thrown a bad pitch. When I got back to the dugout, I asked Hal Smith, who was my catcher, and he said right off that it could not have been improved on.

"I'm sure there're all sorts of stories like that. I remember once that Dick Sisler, the pitcher, came over to us from the American League in a winter trade and he sort of scoffed at those Aaron tales we told him. When you have someone like Aaron in your league you spend a lot of time bragging about him—perhaps so that when he hits a home run you can slough it off: 'I told you so; see?' Well, Sisler didn't believe any of this stuff. He kept telling us what it was like to pitch to Mickey Mantle, how *he* was the sort of guy who really scared you when he stood in the batter's box. Finally, in the exhibition season, Sisler got a chance to pitch to Aaron. The game was in Bradenton, Florida, and on Sisler's first pitch to him, a breaking ball, Aaron hit a foul line drive over the clubhouse, which is 450 feet away. It went out there on the line—just a terrible thing for any pitcher to see, even if it was foul. At the end of the inning Sisler came back to the dugout and he was saying, 'All right. All right. OK. OK'—like you say when you're convinced and you don't want to hear about it no more."

Dixie Walker, who was a Braves' batting coach at one time, and National League batting champion in 1944, used to stand in the shower and gaze at Aaron, his body glistening in the steam across the room, to try to figure out where this sort of power came from. "There's nothing you can tell by his size," he once said. "All I know is that he has the best wrists I've ever seen on a batter. He swings the bat faster than anyone else, it's as simple as that, and that's why the ball *jumps* the way it does."

That was what the baseball people marveled at when they talked about Aaron's batting—his wrists, the strength and quickness of them which produced a home-run trajectory like that of a good four-iron shot in golf—like drives quite unlike the towering lofty shots of a Mantle or Babe Ruth, whose blasts very often were coming straight down when they dropped out of the sky into the seats.

Bob Skinner, who coaches the Pittsburgh Pirates in the National League, once described the trajectory of an Aaron home run with convincing clarity: "The ball starts out on a line and the shortstop jumps for it, just over his fingertips, and then the left fielder jumps for it, just over *his* glove, and the ball keeps rising on that line and whacks up against the slats of a seat in the stands. The two fielders both figured they had a chance of catching that ball, except none of them realized how fast it was rising."

This reminds one, of course, of the famous hyperbolic description of a Rogers Hornsby home run which went between the pitcher's legs and kept on rising in a line over second base and then the center fielder and, for all I know, out over the center-field clock. But I have heard any number of players say they have seen infielders leap for an Aaron hit powered by those incredible wrists that went out on a line and landed beyond the wall.

THE PITCHER HAS GOT ONLY A BALL. I'VE GOT A BAT. SO THE PERCENTAGE IN WEAPONS IS IN MY FAVOR, AND I LET THE FELLOW WITH THE BALL DO THE FRETTING.

—HANK AARON

Atlanta Braves' Bison Burgers

At Turner Stadium in Atlanta, owner Ted Turner provides a little extra for fans—fresh bison meat directly from his own Montana ranch. Ted knows what he's doing with bison meat: It's leaner than beef and makes an absolutely perfect burger for a hot summer day.

1. Combine all the ingredients in a large bowl and mix until well blended.

2. Divide into eight balls and shape into patties.

3. Grill over medium coals about 4 to 6 minutes per side until the burgers are browned and the middle is no longer pink.

Makes 8 burgers.

2 pounds ground bison

2 tablespoons ketchup

2 tablespoons mustard

2 tablespoons hot sauce

1 teaspoon Worcestershire sauce

1 teaspoon salt

½ teaspoon ground pepper

TRADING CARDS & BOBBLE HEADS:
BASEBALL COLLECTIBLES

★ At the turn of the 20th century, baseball cards were created to help sell cigarettes, and then candy and clothing. In 1933 the now classic gum-and-card combination was created by the Goudey Gum Company. For a penny, you got a card and a stick of gum.

★ April 3 is National Trading Card Day.

★ The world's most expensive baseball card—is the $1.265 million PSA NM-MT 8 T206 Honus Wagner. The lore surrounding the scarcity of this 1909 Honus Wagner card is attributed to the baseball player's objection to being used to promote tobacco. Wagner halted production of the card. The story, combined with the few cards actually printed, created its rarity.

From 1954 through 1956, the first three cards of all-time home-run king Hank Aaron sported the same photo. The final year Topps used the photo, the card also included an action shot, supposedly of Aaron sliding into home—but it was actually a famous pulp magazine photo of Willie Mays.

J. R. Burdick, "the world's greatest card collector ever known" (as stated on his tombstone) and editor and publisher of *American Card Catalog*, spent the last 16 years of his life organizing his collection of more than 300,000 cards for the Metropolitan Museum of Art in New York City.

The bat that Mark McGwire used to hit his 70th home run of the 1998 season sold for nearly $3 million to comic book mogul Todd McFarlane.

Ty Cobb's dentures were auctioned in 1999 for $7,475.

Barry Halper is known for having the greatest private collection of baseball collectibles, totaling more than 2,500 items. When it was auctioned off at Sotheby's in 1999, the total take was over $21.8 million. The auction included the only jersey signed by Ty Cobb, the 1920 signed agreement trading Babe Ruth from the Red Sox to the Yankees, and the cleats worn by Pete Rose when he broke the National League record for most hits.

Bobble heads were first imported from Japan in the '50s and '60s, but didn't become a huge collectible until the '80s. In recent years, the craze for the plastic figures that bob has begun again. In 2001, fans camped outside the Mariners stadium to get free Ichiro Suzuki Bobble Head dolls.

The gum in the Topps trading card packs was notoriously hard, but for a reason. It was shoved into packs by machines, and anything softer would have crumbled under the pressure.

NOTES FROM A BASEBALL DREAMER

BY ROBERT MAYER

Sparks splattered out of the dark ceiling like electric fire-flies. I zoomed in and out of traffic on the oval surface. I was driving a bumper car, my favorite amusement park attraction, but I did not like getting bumped, did not care to slam into others. A hook-slider, a bailer-outer, in the Coney Island of my youth,

It was the last weekend in June, school had let out the day before, we were on our traditional family outing to the other end of the city. To the farthest corner of Brooklyn. We climbed out of the bumper cars and walked along the boardwalk, saw the dark Atlantic rolling onto the beach, stopped for hot dogs and french fries at Nathan's, played miniature golf in the sweet salt air, passed advertisements and shills for freak shows featuring snake charmers, sword swallowers, bearded ladies, and assorted other aberrations that I did not care to see or imagine. Finally my brother and I and a

bunch of the other kids went into a penny arcade. While the bigger guys played pinball games, I spotted a baseball card machine.

Some of the boys on the block, David Portman in particular, would buy pack after pack of bubble gum, throwing away the brittle gum but keeping the smallish baseball cards. That always seemed a waste to me. I preferred the postcard-sized cards that you bought for a penny each out of a machine. The cards were sepia. They had no information or statistics on the back, but that didn't matter: I could keep as many statistics as I needed in my head. It was the pictures that counted (and the facsimile signatures), those large soft images, Carl Furillo finishing his swing, Pee Wee Reese bending to scoop a grounder, Preacher Roe pitching. Most of the batters, in fact, were finishing their swings, as I recall, not captured with the bat out over the plate—probably because the extended bat would not fit on the vertical card. This occurs to me only now.

There were card machines in the candy stores near P.S. 70. Some of the kids bought cowboy cards—Bob Steele, Hopalong Cassidy; some bought movie star cards—Bette Davis, Barbara Stanwyck. But baseball was my only vice. And now here was a machine at Coney Island, way out in Brooklyn, with all the attendant possibilities of a new selection of cards: fewer doubles, more originals. I took a penny from my pocket and placed it in the coin slot, pushed the silver metal handle all the way in, slowly pulled out, my heart pounding with the excitement at who the player might be. I don't remember, now, who it was. What I remember, what was astounding at that moment, was that two cards came out instead of one. This had never happened to me before. The cards must have been stuck together, I thought. What luck! I fed another penny into the machine. To my amazement another two cards came out. I tried again. And again. With five pennies I now held ten penny baseball cards in my hands. The unexpected provender of the Coney gods.

My brother and the others came to see what I was doing. I showed them. Two cards for a penny, every time. My brother pushed me out of the way. He tried a penny of his own. Two cards. He tried another penny. Two cards. All of them crowded around now, excited, yet trying to be quiet, not wanting to attract attention, filling their hands with this bargain. I, the youngest and smallest, had been shuffled to the rear, out of the inner circle.

Here I must pause momentarily for a warning. What follows is not for the squeamish. But I have determined in this baseball memoir to pull no punches. Only the strong need read on.

Wandering through the arcade, aimless, alone, I suddenly found myself face to face with a fat belly, with a dirty apron. The apron had large pockets, which hung heavy with coins. Above it the unshaved face of a large man loomed. I hesitated, then tugged at the fat man's apron.

"What do you want?"

"That machine over there," I said, excited, a cub reporter with a scoop, the cub reporter, perhaps, that I would later become. "It's giving out two baseball cards for a penny, instead of one."

"Is that so?" the fat man said,

He patted my light brown hair with appreciation. He strode toward the machine, pushed through the knot of my slavering friends, pushed my brother away from the machine. He took a penny from one of his heavy pockets, shoved it in the machine, pulled the silver handle. Two baseball cards came out. He tried a second time, with the same result.

"That's all, beat it," he said to my brother and the others.

"What do you mean, beat it?" my brother asked.

The fat man produced a gray canvas bag. He pulled it over the machine, as if he were blindfolding a prisoner at the gallows, and he tied the bottom of the bag with a cord.

"The machine's broken. No more cards today. Beat it."

His look turned mean. He was prepared to get physical if the guys didn't move. They seethed out into the bright glare of the boardwalk. The sun shone directly on me, like a spotlight in a police station.

My brother looked at me. "You told him! Why the hell did you tell him?"

"Because the machine was broken."

"Idiot! Stupid schmuck!" And he punched me in the shoulder, hard, with a knuckle protruding, the only time he hit me hard in my life. It hurt like hell.

The others, too, looked at me. Then they turned and walked away, disgusted. I stood alone in a warm puddle of moral uncertainty. All I had done was tell the truth! But in so doing I had become the bearded lady, the two-headed calf, the freak show I dared not witness.

Why I did it I cannot say. Perhaps, by the time I was eight, my parents had already instilled in me some ancient Hebraic notion of absolute rectitude. Or perhaps, as my brother said, I was merely a schmuck.

I still can feel today the touch of the fat man's chubby hand on my hair. As if it was a violation.

And that is only half the agony.

I continued to collect the penny baseball cards throughout my youth, paying a full cent for each one after, one chiseled round portrait of Lincoln for every Gus Zernial and Phil Cavaretta and Hoot Evers. In those days they were the only way to learn what the players looked like, especially players from other cities or the other league, whom you never got to see on the field. One year I did make an exception: I started collecting one set of nickel-a-pack bubble gum cards. I don't recall the brand, but the small, squarish cards were black and white, which I liked, and unlike most cards, the accompanying pink bubble gum was softer than a manhole cover. It wasn't anywhere near the quality of the Fleer's Double Bubble we sidewalk connoisseurs preferred, but it would do. There were forty-eight baseball cards in this particular set, and within a few months one summer I had acquired forty-seven of them. Only Buddy Kerr was missing. Nickel after nickel went for more cards in search of the Giants' shortstop. Nickel after nickel he remained elusive. I went to a Giant-Dodger game at the Polo Grounds, proved to myself that Buddy Kerr did in fact exist, saw him in the flesh. But I never obtained his card. I never even saw his card. I suspect now, in the well-honed cynicism of my years, that they never printed any—well, perhaps one; that Buddy Kerr was somehow chosen to be the Holy Grail we nickel-dropping urchins would never obtain, the bottomless black hole in our childhood galaxy.

A red rubber band wrapped tightly around the set—I was one card short of a deck, then as now—I placed the forty-seven cards in a cardboard box and went back to collecting the postcard size. Sometimes I would trade cards with my friends, sometimes we would flip cards, sometimes we would toss them against a wall (closest to the wall wins), sometimes, using a clothespin, we would fasten the cards to the wheels of our bicycles, which made the spinning spokes roar like a motorcycle. But these diversions I would indulge in only with my doubles. My singles I would not gamble with. When I was twelve years old, my family moved from our apartment in the West Bronx to a house my parents bought in the Pelham Parkway section. My box of baseball cards—it was a multicolored box that had once held jars of finger paints—I placed on a shelf in my closet as I turned my attention to the homework of junior high school, to my fear of the opposite sex, to the pimple which like some unwelcome guest perpetually revisited the point of my nose, to all the other mysteries of adolescence. The box of cards remained at the top of the closet throughout my high school years, throughout college.

It was around this time in the lives of most men that their treasured baseball cards disappeared, never to be seen again. For some it happened when they were away at college, learning the lingo of their future professions. For others it happened when they were in the service, defending their country's honor, its military-industrial complex, whatever. Not so in my case. In my case the wound was self-inflicted.

I was twenty-two years old. I had just taken my first long-term newspaper job. I had fallen in love for the first time. And I decided it was time to grow up. This meant, in the madness of my ardor, two things. First, it meant letting my hair grow out. Since the age of twelve I had worn my hair in a crew cut, a brush cut. I was world class. My hair was so thick and full that every time I went to Rudy, my favorite barber on Eastchester Avenue, he would unwrap a newly sharpened pair of scissors. He would use them to trim my crew cut. When he was done, he would toss them into the drawer of scissors that needed to be sharpened again. My hair wasn't merely cute, it was tough. And it was me. It stands up firm and proud in my high school graduation picture. It does the same in my college graduation picture. It was part of my identity. But now I was in the real world, and in love, and it was time to grow up. I let my crew cut grow out. But that action was fairly painless. It did not seem to complete my rite of passage. It did not assuage the part of my soul that knew I could not remain a little boy. A further task was demanded, something more painful, more drastic. And I knew what it was. One dark night I poked around in the top of the closet of the small room I had long since outgrown. I found the box that had once held finger paints. I wiped off the years of dust, first with my hands, then with a paper towel. I opened the box, and in it, neatly stacked, neatly preserved, were my hundreds of sepia baseball cards. Pee Wee and Duke, Gil and Jackie, Roy, Reach, all the others. Still in perfect condition. A rubber band marked off a small pack of doubles. Perhaps, I thought, if I just threw *those* away…But a stern inner voice said no. The stern inner voice said it was time

to do away with childish things. With a minimum of ceremony I closed the box, carried it down the stairs and out to the street, where our garbage can stood. Like a burial at sea, but without so much as a prayer of farewell, I slid my baseball cards into the trash. Then I turned and walked back to my house under the stars. I had become an adult.

Or so I thought.

The memories those cards would conjure today are priceless. And how much money would they be worth? I have no idea. I have never tried to find out. I dare not speculate. Hundred of dollars, for sure. Thousands, most likely. Tens of thousands is not out of the question in the strange, but burgeoning baseball card market.

But my cards are gone to limbo, like most men's childhood cards. With this one burning difference: I was cheated of the lifelong pleasure of blaming it on my mother.

And what of the inner child that I was trying to kill off? It lives inside me still. Crying, *Schmuck!!!*

AS I SAY, I NEVER FEEL
MORE AT HOME IN AMERICA
THAN AT A BALL GAME BE
IT IN PARK OR IN SANDLOT.
BEYOND THIS I KNOW NOT.
AND DARE NOT.

—ROBERT FROST

LITTLE LEAGUE IS CONSIDERED an essential part of growing up in America. Everyone from Bruce Springsteen to President George W. Bush to Kareem Abdul-Jabbar has played on a Little League team. But in 1938, there was no organized club for young boys to learn the game that was sweeping the country. Carl Stotz of Williamsport, Pennsylvania, recognized that his nephews, both too young to join the popular American Legion teams, were missing an opportunity to learn sportsmanship and teamwork. He wanted to change that.

BOYS OF SUMMER: THE LITTLE LEAGUE

With the help of his wife and neighbors, he experimented with field sizes and base paths that would be appropriate for preteen boys. In 1939, Carl began looking for sponsors in the community for his league—and was rejected by fifty-six businesses. Finally he found three that would agree to pay the $30 fee to form the first teams of Little League—Lycoming Dairy, Lundy Lumber, and Jumbo Pretzel—and paid the rest of the league costs out of his own pocket. The first official Little League game was played on June 6, 1939, with Lundy Lumber topping Lycoming Dairy, 23–8. Allen Yearick of Lycoming Dairy remembers his favorite part of joining the league: "The uniforms . . . we had socks, we had shirts, we had pants. . . . One cannot tell how a little boy can be so happy over getting something and becoming part of something."

The success of the first season inspired the community to get more involved. Little League was becoming such a positive addition to the town, City Hall allowed Stotz to build a field along a busy road at Max M. Brown Memorial Park in 1941, attracting more visitors to each game. Adult volunteerism grew and became essential to the league, with volunteers handling everything from managing teams and umpiring games to painting fences and running concession stands. One volunteer dad, Mac McCloskey, filled in for a missing scorekeeper in 1940, and went on to keep score for every Williamsport Little League game until 1967, a total of 1,327 consecutive games.

With the word of mouth about the league traveling, nearby towns began to develop their own teams, and a World Series was established in 1947. Once again, the community rallied for the boys, with the Williamsport Tigers lending their locker rooms and showers, a nearby church offering meals, and local volunteers becoming "team hosts" for out-of-town boys. The Maynard Midgets won the tournament, defeating the Lock Haven All Stars 16–7.

The next year, Stotz was asked to bring Little League teams to a town 25 miles south of Williamsport for an exhibition game. In the stands that night was a senior editor on vacation from *The Saturday Evening Post*. As a result, the article "Small Boy's Dream Come True" was written, skyrocketing the league to a national stage. Newsreels were shown from the Little League tournament, and excitement built around the country for organized baseball. By 1952, there were 1,500 programs running in the United States. A year later, Joey Jay, a former Little Leaguer, became the first player to move on to the major leagues, with the Milwaukee Braves.

The league was never just about baseball; it always took its homegrown values and rules seriously. Since its conception, Little League had been integrated, with its first all-black team joining

154

in 1939. When the board discovered in 1955 that 61 all-white teams in South Carolina were refusing to play the state's one all-black team, all 61 teams were disqualified from tournament play, sending a message that Little League would not tolerate racism on the field.

International teams have been involved in the World Series since 1952, but none made an impression like the 1957 team from Monterrey, Mexico. They arrived at the airport for the World Series carrying paper bags for luggage, all considerably smaller than their American counterparts. When asked if the bigger size of the other teams was intimidating, first baseman Ricardo Trevino remarked, "We have to play them, not carry them." Days later, pitcher Angel Macias pitched the first perfect game in a championship, making his team the first non-U.S. team to win the World Series. Other teams have created a stir by winning the World Series as well. When a team from Staten Island won in 1964, New York threw them a ticker-tape parade. In 1969, Taiwan won its first Little League World Series title (the country would go on to win a total of 17), becoming the first team in Taiwan's history to win anything internationally. Taiwan treated them like royalty, enrolling the players in better schools and placing their likeness on a stamp.

Little League is now one of the world's largest youth sports programs, with over 200,000 teams in more than 100 countries. Since 2001, Little League Tee Ball has been played regularly on the South Lawn of the White House. It is part of America's conscience, instilling in generation after generation the importance of fair play and doing your best, win or lose.

Little League in Williamsport, Pennsylvania.

Right Field

BY WILLY WELCH

Saturday summers when I was a kid,
we'd run to the schoolyard and here's what we did:
pick out the captains and choose up the teams,
it was always a measure of my self esteem.
Cause the fastest, the strongest played shortstop and first,
the last ones they picked were the worst.
I never needed to ask, it was sealed,
I just took up my place in right field.

Playing right field, it's easy you know,
you can be awkward, you can be slow,
So I'm here in right field,
Watching the dandelions grow.

Playing right field can be lonely and dull,
little leagues never have lefties that pull,
I'd dream of the day they would hit one my way,
they never did, but still I would pray,
that I'd make a fantastic catch on the run,
and not lose the ball in the sun.
Then I'd awake from this long reverie,
And pray that the ball never came out to me.

Off in the distance, the game's dragging on,
there are strikes on the batter, some runners are on.
I don't know the inning, I've forgotten the score.
The whole team is yelling and I don't know what for.
And suddenly everyone's looking at me,
my mind has been wandering, what can it be?
They point to the sky and I look up above,
and a baseball falls into my glove!

Here in right field, it's important you know,
you gotta know how to catch, you gotta know how to throw,
that's why I'm here in right field,
watching the dandelions grow.

YOU HAVE TO HAVE A LOT OF THE LITTLE BOY IN YOU TO PLAY BASEBALL FOR A LIVING.

—ROY CAMPANELLA

HOT TO TROT WITH NO PLACE TO GO

BY RICK REILLY

You know why kids don't play baseball anymore? Because they took down the fences.

It's the era of the dread multiuse field. Every kid's diamond now has to share its centerfield with three other fields and a tai chi class. This way, come spring and fall, the park can be turned into (cough, hack, spit) soccer fields.

What fun is baseball without a fence? Without a fence you can't hit a real home run, and without a real home run you can't do the *home run trot*, which is one of the last truly American joys.

I love the *home run trot*. The longer, the better. Did you see Rickey Henderson's *home run trot* the other night in Baltimore? You could've washed and waxed a 1973 Plymouth Barracuda in the time it took him to get around the bases. Henderson turns a home run into an HBO special. First, he pulls at his jersey. Then he slaps his helmet. Twice. Then he hip-hops in the box a few times, and, finally, he takes off on his epic journey, going so wide around first and third that he nearly steps in both dugouts. Generally, Henderson gets around the bases just a hair faster than a man laying sod.

Pete Rose used to fly around the bases as though he had a pot of soup boiling over somewhere. Occasionally he'd touch a bag, but he wasn't a stickler about it. Frank Robinson told him, "Kid, you better leave those homers to those of us who can act them out."

Mickey Mantle always ran with his head down in shame, as if he were eight years old and had just put one through a stained glass window. Babe Ruth ran with little mincing steps, as though he were trying not to step on cracks. Dave Parker used to trot with fingers pointed like pistols.

Right now is a great time to be alive if you're hot for trots, on account of sluggers are hitting home runs every three minutes. Mark McGwire is on pace to hit 311 this year. McGwire has a very humble trot, but he does the coolest thing before he starts: The instant he connects, he flips the bat away, end over end, like a toothpick, as if to say, "Well, there's no use having that around anymore."

Just the idea of the trot is wonderful. Here a man is being allowed to gallivant from one base to the next—real estate that is fraught with peril and angst in every other moment of the game—at his leisure! As he does this, the fielders have to just stand there, hands on hips, and watch, clench-jawed, as he mocks them with his lazy left turns.

You could retype Shakespeare's sonnets into Sanskrit in the time it takes Barry Bonds to get around, yet he's still faster than Oscar Gamble was. One day Ken Griffey Sr. was in the New York Yankees'

clubhouse in Minnesota when teammate Gamble smashed one out. Griffey dashed out of the clubhouse, around a corner and down a tunnel, figuring he'd get to home plate just as Gamble was crossing it. Except when Griffey got to the top step of the dugout, Gamble was still waiting for the bat boy to come get his bat. Why rush?

Great trotters are men of courage because they know they might get an earful of cowhide next time up. Yet they carry on. Jeffrey (Hackman) Leonard let his left arm hang limp and leaned toward the pitcher as he ran, like some disabled Cessna. Reggie Jackson would pose long enough to strike a decent oil painting.

The trot is part of the game's very fabric. Remember the look on the face of the death-threatened Hank Aaron when the two fans caught up to him between second and third on number 715? Remember Jimmy Piersall going around backward on his 100th? Do you realize the greatest *home run trot* ever was done on one leg—Kirk Gibson's, after his heroic pinch-hit 1988 Series shocker against the Oakland A's?

Look, baseball is a game of simple pleasures. I coach a team in the Catholic Youth League, and when one of my kids slams a huge one, he doesn't get the glory of a trot. He sprints madly around the bases in case the kid in left has somehow grown a catapult for a right arm and can throw him out from some lady's purse on Field Number 14.

Please, Mr. Parks and Rec Director, if you love baseball, fence us in. Home runs and childhood are over way too soon.

Going Going Gone Cookies

1 cup (2 sticks) butter, at room temperature

1 cup sugar

2 eggs

1 teaspoon vanilla extract

3 cups flour

No baseball theme party is complete without a treat that looks like, that's right, a ball. Our recipes combine the best sugar cookies with a simple red frosting for stitching.

1. Cream together the butter and sugar. Beat in the eggs and add the vanilla. Add the flour and mix well. Refrigerate at least 2 hours.

2. Preheat the oven to 375 degrees and line baking sheets with parchment paper.

3. Roll out the dough on a lightly floured surface (marble or wood) and cut with a cookie cutter. Transfer the cookies to cookie sheets with a spatula. Bake approximately 10 minutes. When the cookies are beginning to brown, remove them from the oven and slide the parchment off the baking sheet. When the cookies have cooled a bit, slide them off the parchment. Cool the cookie sheets before using them again. Wait until the cookies are completely cool before icing.

1 package (16 ounces) confectioners' sugar

3 organic egg whites

1 tablespoon white vinegar

Red food coloring

Makes 3 to 5 dozen cookies, depending on size and thickness.

The Perfect Stitch Icing

1. Place the confectioners' sugar in a mixing bowl.

2. In a separate bowl, beat the egg whites lightly with a fork. Add them to the sugar and beat 1 minute with an electric mixer on its lowest speed. Add the vinegar and beat 2 more minutes at high speed, or until the mixture is stiff and glossy.

3. Add a few drops of food coloring and stir. Continue adding coloring until a nice red is achieved.

4. Using a knife or a frosting bag, draw two lines down each cookie, like stitching on a baseball.

5. Enjoy!

WHO'S ON FIRST:
FIRSTS IN BASEBALL

1845 The first formal team—the Knickerbocker Club of New York—was formed by Alexander Cartwright.

1857 The game changes from a first-team-to-21-points to a nine-inning format.

1871 Batting averages begin to be recorded for players.

1876 A small glove with padding is worn in the game for the first time to soften the blow of catching a ball.

1877 Formal playing schedules are announced in advance for the first time in order to allow fans time to plan for their teams' home games.

1887 Batters are no longer allowed to call for the type of pitch—high or low—that they want.

1900 A new pentagon-shaped home plate replaces the diamond-shaped model.

1910 William Taft is the first president to throw out the first pitch on Opening Day.

1911 The era of "deadball" baseball comes to an end, as the cork-and-rubber filled baseball is introduced to the delight of fans, who now see homerun averages skyrocket.

168

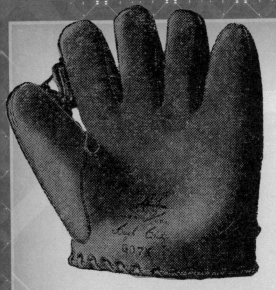

1915 The Yankees wear pinstripes on their uniforms for the first time.

1929 The first public address system in the major leagues is used for the Giants July 5th game.

1931 It becomes mandatory for all teams in the American League to wear numbers on their uniforms.

1939 Lou Gehrig is the first player to have his number retired.

1954 Players may no longer leave their gloves on the field while their team is at bat.

1957 Batting helmets are made mandatory.

1975 Catfish Hunter is the first player to be declared a free agent. The Yankees win the bidding war and Hunter wears the pinstripes for the next five seasons.

1976 The first designated hitter is used in a World Series game—Dan Driessen of the Cincinnati Reds.

1978 The first division playoff game is held, with the Yankees beating the Red Sox 5-4 at Fenway Park.

1985 The League Championship Series changes to a best-four-of-seven format.

1991 The Atlanta Braves become the first team to go from the worst in the league one year to best the next—also referred to as jumping from "worst to first."

1994 Due to a season-ending strike, 1994 is the first year since 1871 when no World Series takes place.

2001 Cub Sammy Sosa becomes the first player to hit 60 home runs in a season for three straight seasons.

BABE RUTH

BABE RUTH IS WIDELY REGARDED as the player who saved baseball. After the 1919 Black Sox scandal, Ruth changed baseball into a sport where consistent home runs were expected and a life in the public eye was just part of the game. George Herman Ruth Jr. was born February 6, 1895, in Baltimore, Maryland, to George and Kate Ruth. Both parents worked at the local tavern, often leaving George alone at a young age. By seven, George was such a handful that his father brought him to St. Mary's Industrial School for Boys. The orphanage's Catholic missionaries were given custody of George, who cared for him during his 12 years there. His parents and sister rarely visited, and the school found him to be difficult to handle.

While at the orphanage, George was taken under the wing of Brother Matthias, who helped him learn the game of baseball and gave him the encouragement that he had never been given at home. George played for St. Mary's varsity baseball team, and his extraordinary talent was apparent to all who saw him play.

At the age of 19, George was signed by the Baltimore Orioles, the Red Sox's minor-league team. Manager Jack Dunn saw a lot of potential in Ruth, so his teammates nicknamed him Jack's newest "Babe," a moniker that stuck throughout his career.

Two years later, Babe was playing in his first Wold Series with the Red Sox. In his first game of the Series, he set a record that still stands: He pitched 14 innings, 13 of which were scoreless. It's the longest complete game in World Series history. With the Red Sox, Babe won World Championships in 1915, 1916, and 1918. After they traded him to the Yankees

during the postseason of 1919, the Red Sox would go 86 years before they won another championship. This streak was referred to as "the Curse of the Bambino."

Babe and the sport of baseball soared to new heights during his years with the New York Yankees. In 1920, he smashed his home run count, going from 29 the previous year to 54. With his gregarious personality and home run records, Babe drew so many fans to the Polo Grounds that the Yankees could afford to build a new stadium, which opened in 1923 and earned the affectionate nickname "The House That Ruth Built." On Opening Day at Yankee Stadium, Babe knocked one into the stands, to the delight of the fans. He ended the season by leading the Yankees to their first World Series victory.

As his fame on the field grew, the stories of Ruth's personal life caught people's interest, too. He was known as a man who lived life the same way he played baseball—large. Rumors circulated that he once ate as many as 18 hot dogs in one sitting, and that his breakfasts consisted of 18-egg omelets and beer. His drinking, womanizing, and rule breaking often put a damper on his career, causing brief suspensions and hospitalizations, but Babe always bounced back. Once on a game day, he was arrested for speeding in New York City. As game time drew near, Babe was allowed to change into his uniform in his cell while he waited for his release. He made it to the stadium on time, and the Yankees won the game 4–3.

Babe reached his peak in 1927, when he hit 60 home runs in one season, a record that stood for another 34 years. Another landmark moment happened in during Game 4 of the 1932

World Series. Babe reputedly pointed to the outfield and then hit a homer there on his next swing to win the championship. In his 22 years as a player, Babe hit 714 home runs, won seven championships, and became one of the illustrious "First Five" inducted into the Hall of Fame. When he died in 1948, his body was placed in the entrance of Yankee Stadium; more than 100,000 people came to pay their respects to the Sultan of Swat.

Babe Ruth's Farewell to Baseball Address

April 27, 1947, Yankee Stadium, New York

Thank you very much, ladies and gentlemen.

You know how bad my voice sounds—well it feels just as bad.

You know this baseball game of ours comes up from the youth. That means the boys.

And if you're a boy and grow up and know how to play ball, then you come to the boys you see representing themselves today in your national pastime.

The only real game—I think—in the world is baseball.

As a rule, some people think that if you give them a football, or a baseball, or something like that—naturally they're athletes right away.

But you can't do that in baseball.

You've gotta start from way down [at] the bottom, when you're six or seven years of age. You can't wait until you're fifteen or sixteen. You gotta let it grow up with you. And if you're successful, and you try hard enough, you're bound to come out on top—just like these boys have come to the top now.

There's been so many lovely things said about me, and I'm glad that I've had the opportunity to thank everybody.

Thank you.

175

BROOKLYNS LOSE

BY WILLIAM HEUMAN

It's one of those long, drawn-out games at Ebbets Field, and it's not over till nearly six o'clock. We come out hot and tired, and with a little headache— you know how it is after a game—and the kid says he wants a hot dog.

"I like the long ones, Pop," he says.

You know the kind they sell outside the park at those little hot-dog stands, long and skinny and rubbery.

"Never mind," I tell him.

We're hurrying for the trolley car, and the big crowd is pouring out of the exit gates. It's almost six o'clock and Madge has the supper on the table, and I can see her fuming, and the kid's talking about hot dogs.

"Forget it," I tell him.

Who thinks about food when the Dodgers lose? You sit there for nearly three and a half hours and you try to root them home. You're with them every minute, every play, and you have it in the bag, and then it's gone over the wall.

"That was some home run," the kids says.

"Shut up," I tell him. "Keep quiet."

"Well, it was good, Pop. Way out toward center field."

A home run in the last inning which wins the ball game and sends the Brooklyns down to defeat is never a good home run. What the kid means is that it was well hit, I admit that. I'm a Brooklyn fan, but I admit that. The ball travels maybe four hundred feet before it clears the fence in right center, so it's a good hit. All right, but don't rub it in. Three and a half hours I sit there in the bleachers on a hot day and we lose anyway. So what's good about it?

A guy on the trolley says to me, "They shoulda passed him, that Kluszewski."

"Alston didn't wanna put the winning run on base," I tell him. "That's baseball. You play the averages."

"He didn't put Kluszewski on, neither," this guy says, grinning. "Klu hit it an' kept goin'."

This guy jokes, yet. This is a time for jokes when you have a ball game sewed up eight-to-seven in the ninth, and you lose it with a home-run ball.

I look out the window, and the guy says, "So tomorrow's another day."

I don't even look at him. That kind of guy I don't look at.

You don't mind losing a ball game now and then, but when you lose to Cincinnati it hurts, especially when you got it sewed up, and especially in September and you're way out of first place and that old lost column can murder you.

The kid's getting wise here. He's eleven now, and I've had him down to a lot of ball games, and he argues baseball with the other kids on the block.

He says now, "They shoulda took Oiskin out."

"Never mind," I tell him. "Forget about it."

Why can't they let it drop? It's over and we lose it, so it goes down in the records, and you never change the records, not even if the Russians come over and take this country. It's down in the books.

So maybe Alston should have taken Erskine out, and maybe put in Johnny Podres, and Podres walks three-four guys and it's over anyway, and Alston's a dope again. He should have left Erskine in.

I don't like to second-guess the manager. The guy is out there with his job to do, and he knows more about it than anybody else. Just like me at the shop. In the shop I know my job and I do it. I don't like a guy coming round and telling me it might work out better some other way.

178

I'm just saying, though, that if it was me in Alston's shoes I'd have had Shuba pinch-hit for Erskine the end of the eighth, and maybe bring in another run or two, so when this big clown belts one over the wall in the ninth we still got the lead. With Erskine out for a pinch hitter I'd have stuck Roe in there for one inning with that slow stuff. It might have been a different game.

Like I say, though, you can't second-guess, and it's silly to work yourself up into a stew because we dropped one. Just forget about it; let it drop.

I hear a guy in the seat behind me say, "They shoulda pulled a squeeze in the seventh with Reese on third. When Dressen was runnin' this club he worked a lot of squeeze plays. We'd of had that extra run, and when Kluszewsik hits that homer it's only tied up, an'—"

You see how they try to dope it out? It's dead; it's in the record books. And who's up when Reese is on third and one away? Gil Hodges is up, and Gil is a long-ball hitter. Since when do you ask your long-ball hitter to bunt? That guy behind me is crazy. Any kind of fly ball would have brought Reese in. So Hodges struck out; so Alston knew he was gonna strike out?

If it was me I'd have had Reese try to steal home

when it was two out. This Cincinnati guy was taking a long windup. I'm not telling Alston how to run his ball club, but you can see how it goes around and around inside your head. I've heard of guys going off their trolley arguing points like this.

Madge says when we come into the house at about six-thirty:

"What were you doing—standing outside the field asking for their autographs?"

She has that look on her face. The pots are still on the stove, all covered up, and they've been there for some time, I can see.

"It was a long game," I tell her.

"It's always a long game down there," she says, and the way she says "there" you'd think she was talking of some gin mill somewhere.

She should be married to a heavy drinker or a guy who plays the horses like some of them in the shop. I don't have any bad habits; I have a glass of beer now and then; I go to Ebbets Field. That's wrong?

"Sit down and eat your supper," Madge says.

"Pop wouldn't buy me a hot dog," the kid tells her.

"I'm not surprised," Madge says. "He probably didn't even know you were with him."

"I bought him two in the park," I snap. "He wants another one on the way home. What am I—Rockefeller?"

"He'd have had a better time at Brighton Beach," Madge says as she's banging the pots around on the stove.

"My vacation," I tell her. "Monday we go to the beach. Wednesday we go to the beach. What am I—a seal?"

"Sit down," she says.

I notice that there are four plates set out and I know who the other plate is for. He comes in from the parlor, snapping at his suspenders—the last guy I want to see tonight.

Uncle Nathan is my brother-in-law, a bachelor, and he lives in a rooming house around the corner from us. Every once in a while—and even once is too often—Madge invites him around for supper. I'm practically supporting this guy, and I think that, secretly, he likes the Giants.

"Lost again," Uncle Nathan grins as he sits down opposite me. "Heard it on the radio."

"Again," I tell him acidly. "Don't I know it's again?"

"The Reds," Uncle Nathan says. "The Cincinnati Reds from Cincinnati."

He's a guy who never goes to a ball game, but he can make remarks like that. He don't know first base from second.

"Kluszewski hit a home run and won the game in the ninth inning," the kids says, and I have to hear that over again.

"They should have a man like Kluszewski on first base for Brooklyn," Uncle Nathan says.

"What's wrong with Hodges?" I ask him. "What's wrong with a guy who hits over three hundred and drives in all them runs?"

"Eat your supper," Madge says.

Who feels like eating, especially with Uncle Nathan sitting across from you, smirking? Uncle Nathan is a small, pot-bellied guy with a circle of fuzzy hair around his bald head. All his life he's lived in Brooklyn, twenty minutes from the field, and never saw a game. That's a citizen!

"Who was it beat them this afternoon?" Uncle Nathan says. "I never heard of the guy."

"How many guys you ever heard of in baseball?" I ask him.

"Eat your supper, Joe," Madge says. "You'd all be a lot better off if you spent your time on something more educational."

I could make some remarks about that, too, but I don't. I got arguments up to the neck, already. Education. What's education but knowing something, and what's better to know than Brooklyn wins?

"Hear the Giants won this afternoon," Uncle Nathan says, without looking up from his plate. "Three-to-one over the Cardinals. They got it made."

"They'll fade in the stretch," I say. "They'll drop a few, and we'll catch them in the last week. We got a three-game series here, remember."

Imagine a guy talking about the Giants down here in Flatbush. A guy like that is crazy. He should be arrested.

I don't eat much tonight because I'm not hungry, and I guess I don't say much, either, because Madge says, as she's bringing out the dessert:

"All afternoon you yell your head off at the game. When you come home, you shut up like a clam."

"What's to say?" I ask her. "I gotta talk every minute?"

"He'd be talkin' plenty," Uncle Nathan says, "if the Dodgers had won."

I don't even bother to answer.

The kid, sitting next to me at the table, says, "That Kluszewski sure can hit."

Good 'n Hot Pretzels

Whether you're rooting for the Nationals or the A's, the Marlins or the Twins, you'll love these hot pretzels. Sure, baseball might tear your own family between the Mets and the Yankees, but if anything can bring them back together, it's good, wholesome snacks. With a lot of mustard.

1 cup lukewarm water

1 tablespoon yeast

4 tablespoons brown sugar

2 teaspoons sea salt

3 cups all-purpose flour

1 tablespoon baking soda dissolved in 1 cup boiling water

1 egg beaten with 1 teaspoon water in a small bowl

Coarse sea salt

1. Preheat the oven to 425 degrees.

2. Mix the water, yeast, brown sugar, and salt in a large mixing bowl. Add the flour and knead until the dough is smooth (about 3 minutes). Allow the dough to rest in the refrigerator, covered, at least 1 hour, but preferably overnight.

3. Divide the dough into 6 or 12 pieces and roll each piece into a rope.

4. Shape each section into an upside-down U-shape in front of you. Bring the ends together and twist them halfway up, making them look like a tie or ribbon.

5. Flatten the loose ends with your fingers, then bring them up to the top of the pretzel (the top of the upside-down U); press them into the dough to secure. It should now look like a pretzel.

6. Place on a greased cookie sheet.

7. Let the pretzels rise for 30 minutes or until about double in size. Brush with the water–baking soda solution, followed by the egg wash.

8. Sprinkle generously with coarse salt.

9. Bake 12 to 15 minutes or until golden brown.

10. Serve hot, with mustard if desired.

Makes 6 or 12 small pretzels.

THE ROOKIES

- The Rookie of the Year Award—or Jackie Robinson Award, as it became known in 1987—is given to the individual player from each league who has the best rookie season in pitching, hitting, or fielding during his first year of eligibility.

- Eligibility requirements set forth in 1971 by Major League Baseball formally defined *rookie* as a player with less than 130 at-bats, a pitcher with less than 50 innings pitched, or anyone with less than 45 days on any major-league roster.

- During the 1964 season, outfielder Tony Oliva of the Minnesota Twins was the first Rookie of the Year who also earned a batting title. This accomplishment wasn't duplicated until 2001, by Ichiro Suzuki of the Seattle Mariners.

- Mark McGwire of the Oakland A's was the first and only Rookie of the Year who also led the league in home runs, in 1987.

- Only a small number of players have been unanimous winners of the Rookie of the Year Award. They are Frank Robinson ('56), Orlando Cepeda ('58), Willie McCovey ('59), Carlton Fisk ('72), Vince Coleman ('85), Benito Santiago ('87), Mark McGwire ('87), Sandy Alomar Jr. ('90), Mike Piazza ('93), Tim Salmon ('93), Raul Mondesi ('94), Derek Jeter ('96), Scott Rolen ('97), Nomar Garciaparra ('97), and Albert Pujols ('01).

- Nicknamed "Jet" for his tremendous speed on the base paths, Sam Jethroe became one of the first Negro League players to break through baseball's color barrier. His first-year performance also earned him National League Rookie of the Year honors in 1950. He was 32 years old that season.

- Vince Coleman has the highest number of stolen bases as a rookie, stealing 110 bases in 1985 while playing for St. Louis.

- In 1984, Dwight Gooden of the New York Mets became the rookie pitcher with the most strikeouts: 276.

- Irv Young of Boston pitched the most innings his rookie year, in 1905: 378.

- The first Rookie of the Year was Jackie Robinson from Brooklyn, in 1947.

Casey at the Bat

Ernest L. Thayer

The outlook wasn't brilliant for the Mudville nine that day;
The score stood four to two with but one inning more to play;
And then, when Cooney died at first, and Barrows did the same,
A sickly silence fell upon the patrons of the game.

A struggling few got up to go, in deep despair. The rest
Clung to that hope which "springs eternal in the human breast";
They thought, If only Casey could get but a whack at that,
We'd put up even money now, with Casey at the bat.

But Flynn preceded Casey, as did also Jimmy Blake,
And the former was a lulu and the latter was a cake;
So, upon that stricken multitude grim melancholy sat,
For there seemed but little chance of Casey's getting to the bat.

But Flynn let drive a single, to the wonderment of all,
And Blake, the much despised, tore the cover off the ball,
And when the dust had lifted and the men saw what had occurred,
There was Jimmy safe at second, and Flynn a-huggin' third.

Then from five thousand throats and more there rose a lusty yell,
It rumbled through the valley; it rattled in the dell;
It knocked upon the mountain and recoiled upon the flat,
For Casey, mighty Casey, was advancing to the bat.

There was ease in Casey's manner as he stepped into his place;
There was pride in Casey's bearing and a smile on Casey's face,
And when, responding to the cheers, he lightly doffed his hat,
No stranger in the crowd could doubt 'twas Casey at the bat.

Ten thousand eyes were on him as he rubbed his hands with dirt;
Five thousand tongues applauded when he wiped them on his shirt.
Then while the writhing pitcher ground the ball into his hip,
Defiance gleamed in Casey's eye, a sneer curled Casey's lip.

And now the leather-covered sphere came hurtling through the air,
And Casey stood a-watching it in haughty grandeur there.
Close by the sturdy batsman the ball unheeded sped.
"That ain't my style," said Casey. "Strike one," the umpire said.

From the benches, black with people, there went up a muffled roar,
Like the beating of the storm-waves on a stern and distant shore.

"Kill him; kill the umpire!" shouted someone from the stand—
And its likely they'd have killed him had not Casey raised his hand.

With a smile of Christian charity great Casey's visage shone;
He stilled the rising tumult; he bade the game go on;
He signaled to the pitcher, and once more the spheroid flew;
But Casey still ignored it, and the umpire said, "Strike two."

"Fraud," cried the maddened thousands, and echo answered fraud;
But one scornful look from Casey, and the audience was awed.
They saw his face grow stern and cold, they saw his muscles strain,
And they knew that Casey wouldn't let that ball go by again.

The sneer is gone from Casey's lip; his teeth are clenched in hate;
He pounds with cruel violence his bat upon the plate.
And now the pitcher holds the ball, and now he lets it go,
And now the air is shattered by the force of Casey's blow.

Oh, somewhere in this favored land the sun is shining bright;
The band is playing somewhere, and somewhere hearts are light,
And somewhere men are laughing, and somewhere children shout;
But there is no joy in Mudville—mighty Casey has struck out.

FROM

SUMMER OF '98:

WHEN HOMERS FLEW, RECORDS FELL, AND BASEBALL RECLAIMED AMERICA

BY MIKE LUPICA

Alex, my seven-year-old, had the Mark McGwire card I'd bought him in the souvenir shop, holding on to it like it was a winning lottery ticket.

Or maybe just a ticket to the whole season, the first that would ever really matter to him, the one that would make him care.

The season starting right now for him, spring training on a Sunday afternoon, McGwire right there in front of him.

The McGwire card was in a plastic case, made to look like a miniature plaque. Alex liked the looks of that. He is the keeper of things in the house. Of my three sons, he is the nester. Next to his bed, on the floor, he lays out autographed balls and bats and caps and trophies and signed photographs and what he calls his "special cards." The walls are now covered with posters of his favorite players, color photographs he has ripped from the sports magazines. Underneath the bed, in drawers, are all his jerseys, with names and numbers on the back. It is the shrine of all his stuff.

McGwire will be a special card, he had said in the store.

"If he breaks the record this year," he said, "I'll know I had this card from the start."

"It's good that it has a cover on it," he said. "You have to take care of your special cards."

This would be the season when baseball would get into his heart, the way baseball still can; the way it always has in this country, for boys like this. Alex would turn eight in April, a few weeks after Opening Day. He would play on his first Little League team. And this would just be the time in his life when the spark was lit for him. It would happen for his brothers, too, just more with him. Things go deep with Alex. In all the best, bright ways, baseball would go deep with him in the summer of 1998.

Like some McGwire home run that would never stop rolling.

It would not just be one thing, between this day in spring training and the end of the World Series. It would not just be the home runs, or all the games the Yankees would win, or the afternoon when he saw Ken Griffey, Jr., and Alex Rodriguez in person for the first time, or the manager of the Mets, Bobby Valentine, coming over to wish him happy birthday when he sat down close to the field at Shea Stadium with his friends.

It would not just be his first team, or uniform, or putting on catcher's gear for the first time, or buying the Mike Piazza mitt with his own money, or making baseball card deals with the adults who own and operate his favorite card stores; or the way he would close his door at night, when he didn't know I was on the other side, and do the imaginary play-by-play of the big-league games he was playing inside his wonderful head:

"There is a long fly ball from Alex Lupica....It could be a home run....It IS a home run!..."

It would not be all the backyard games he invented, usually in the early evening after his supper, Wiffle ball games of home-run derby over the fence around the swimming pool, or all the fly balls I would feed him at the fence, the pressure all on me to make the perfect throw so he could leap against the fence and take an imaginary home run away from someone.

It was all of it, starting now, with the McGwire card in his right hand and McGwire on the field in front of him.

"He's going to hit one today," Alex said to his brothers.

We were in right field at Roger Dean Stadium, the Cardinals' new spring training home in Jupiter, Florida. Cardinals against one of the season's expansion teams, the Tampa Bay Devil Rays. The opponent held no real interest for my kids. Neither did the Cardinals, for that matter. They were here to see McGwire, in this sweet spring training place, everything new and trying to look old, because that is the trend in baseball now, at places like Camden Yards in Baltimore and

Jacobs Field in Cleveland. It was the same in the spring. Places like Jupiter built ballparks like these and lured teams like the Cardinals away from Al Lang Stadium in St. Petersburg, an ancient capital of spring training, as ancient as the population of St. Petersburg.

And Jupiter got lucky, here at Roger Dean, hard by I-95 off Donald Ross Boulevard.

In the spring of '98, Jupiter got McGwire, who had hit 58 home runs for the A's and the Cardinals the year before, who had become the biggest action hero in baseball since Babe Ruth. The stands were full this day because they would be full every day for McGwire, and everyone was here for the reason my sons and I were here:

He might hit one out today.

Maybe he would go deep.

The simplest things always bring us back. The promise of sports, the pull of it, is always the same for fans: We show up wanting this year to be better than last year. And we want to be a part of that. If this year was better than last year for Mark McGwire, even just a little better, a handful of home runs, he would get to 60, which was the best Babe Ruth ever did, back in 1927. A couple more and he would beat Roger Maris's 61, hit for the '61 Yankees. That was the magic number now, for baseball and all sports:

Sixty-one.

Nobody had to tell me.

The spark had been lit for me that summer of '61, the summer of Maris and Mickey Mantle both trying to break Ruth's record. They were together for most of the summer and then Maris had pulled away at the end, finally passing Ruth on the last day of the regular season.

We were living in Oneida, New York, then, about twenty minutes east of Syracuse. Yankee Stadium was five hours away by car, and so it was on the other side of the world for me. My father and I followed Maris and Mantle on the radio, and on the Syracuse television station, Channel 3, that carried some of the Yankee games in those days. No ESPN then. No cable. No color television for us. I remember the season in black-and-white. I turned nine that spring. It was my first season in Little League.

That was my home-run summer, the way this would be a home-run summer for my sons.

I followed Maris and Mantle through the voices of Mel Allen and Phil Rizzuto. There were other voices for the Yankees, and on the Game of the Week. I can only hear Allen and Rizzuto. When I would finally go to bed, exhausting the last possible angle to get one more inning with my father, he would promise to leave me a note on the floor of my room. And would:

Maris hit another one. 42.
Mantle 1-for-4, no home runs.
Yanks, 5–2.

The Greatest

BY DON SCHLITZ

Little boy in a baseball hat
Stands in the field with his ball and bat.
Says, "I am the greatest player of them all."
Puts his bat on his shoulder, and he tosses up his ball.

And the ball goes up and the ball comes down,
Swings his bat all the way around.
The world's so still you can hear the sound.
The baseball falls to the ground.

Now the little boy doesn't say a word.
Picks up his ball; he is undeterred.
Says, "I am the greatest there has ever been."
And he grits his teeth and he tries it again.

And the ball goes up and the ball comes down,
Swings his bat all the way around.
The world's so still you can hear the sound.
The baseball falls to the ground.

200

He makes no excuses,
He shows no fear.
He just closes his eyes and listens to the cheers.

Little boy, he adjusts his hat,
Picks up his ball, stares at his bat.
Says, "I am the greatest, the game is on the line."
And he gives his all one last time.

And the ball goes up like the moon so bright,
Swings his bat with all his might.
The world's as still as still can be,
The baseball falls and that's strike three.

Now it's supper time and his mama calls.
Little boy starts home with his bat and ball.
Says, "I am the greatest, that is a fact,
But even I didn't know I could pitch like that."

Says, "I am the greatest,
That is understood,
But even I didn't know I could pitch that good."

As children, we were not only allowed to play baseball every day, we were expected to. It made us laugh and cry, win and lose; it broke our hearts and made us feel like champions. And it brought everyone together. Baseball was life in those wonderful days.

—John Grisham

NY Giants' Minor League Training Base, Sanford, Florida

Lou Gehrig's
Farewell Speech

July 4, 1939, New York

Fans, for the past two weeks you have been reading about the bad break I got. Yet today I consider myself the luckiest man on the face of this earth. I have been in ballparks for seventeen years and have never received anything but kindness and encouragement from you fans.

Look at these grand men. Which of you wouldn't consider it the highlight of his career just to associate with them for even one day? Sure, I'm lucky. Who wouldn't consider it an honor to have known Jacob Ruppert? Also, the builder of baseball's greatest empire, Ed Barrow? To have spent six years with that wonderful little fellow, Miller Huggins? Then to have spent the next nine years with that outstanding leader, that smart student of psychology, the best manager in baseball today, Joe McCarthy? Sure, I'm lucky.

When the New York Giants, a team you would give your right arm to beat, and vice versa, sends you a gift—that's something. When everybody down to the groundskeepers and those boys in white coats remember you with trophies—that's something. When you have a wonderful mother-in-law who takes sides with you in squabbles with her own daughter—that's something. When you have a father and a mother who work all their lives so you can have an education and build your body—it's a blessing. When you have a wife who has been a tower of strength and shown more courage than you dreamed existed—that's the finest I know.

So I close in saying that I may have had a tough break, but I have an awful lot to live for.

HE WAS HUMBLE, he was kind, he was consistent, and by his own admission he was the luckiest man on earth. A born-and-bred New Yorker, Heinrich Ludwig Gehrig gave his hometown everything he had—and the city has been eternally grateful. On June 19, 1903, two German immigrants, Heinrich and Christina Gehrig, welcomed their son Lou into the world. With her husband ill, Christina worked endlessly to ensure that her only child would have an education. Lou followed his

LOU GEHRIG

mother's dream to Columbia University, where he studied engineering on a football scholarship. Aside from football, he also played first base for the Columbia Nine. In 1923, he was discovered by a scout, and, against his mother's wishes, signed with the Yankees.

Two years later, Lou played his first full season with the Yanks. It didn't take long before he developed a reputation as a consistent threat at the plate. By 1926, Lou was batting over .300, a standard he would meet for the next 12 seasons. Together with his teammate Babe Ruth, they catapulted the team into dynasty status. In 1927, Ruth and Gehrig hit more home runs than all but one other baseball team combined. But Lou's legacy extends beyond the plate; he's often called the best first baseman of his time. With Gehrig in pinstripes, the Yanks went to the World Series in 1926, '27, '28, '32, '36, '37, and '38. They won six out of seven times.

While other players might falter or become disillusioned about playing in the shadow of such teammates as Ruth and, later, Joe DiMaggio, Lou never did. He seemed to flourish with the attention elsewhere, following Ruth in the batting order without ever struggling to perform. In fact, it was this modest, hardworking attitude that gave Gehrig his greatest record. He played for almost 14 years without ever missing a game. The first baseman played through 17 different fractures, a broken thumb and toe, severe back pain, and illnesses to complete his 2,130-consecutive-game streak. For this unbelievable accomplishment, he earned the nickname "the Iron Horse."

In the last years of his career, Gehrig lost his usual spark. He batted under .300, something he hadn't done since 1925. His streak continued, because manager Joe McCarthy wanted to let his captain and star player make his own decision about when he couldn't play anymore. In 1939, Lou knew he wasn't playing well enough to support the team, and for that reason he asked to be benched. It was his job as captain to present the roster, and for the first time he wasn't on it. After that day, he was diagnosed with the rare degenerative disease amyotrophic lateral sclerosis, now more commonly known as Lou Gehrig's disease. The Iron Horse never played baseball again.

On the Fourth of July, 1939, his team held a recognition ceremony at the stadium to commemorate their captain. Lou walked hesitantly up to the microphone and gave the speech he would always be remembered for, citing himself the luckiest man on earth. Once again, Lou Gehrig proved himself to be the ultimate example of a gentleman. To assure that he would be present for one last triumph, the Hall of Fame inducted him that winter, waiving the usual waiting period. Two years later, the Iron Horse passed away. His wife, Eleanor, received flowers from President Roosevelt and more than 1,500 telegrams in sympathy. Lou Gehrig remained, to his last days, the heart of the New York Yankees.

THE METS LOSE AN AWFUL LOT? LISTEN, MISTER. THINK A LITTLE BIT. WHEN WAS THE LAST TIME YOU WON ANYTHING OUT OF LIFE?

—JIMMY BRESLIN

THE NATURAL

BY BERNARD MALAMUD

As the cab pulled up before the hotel, a wild-eyed man in shirtsleeves, hairy-looking and frantic, rushed up to them.

"Any of you guys Roy Hobbs?"

"That's him," Pop said grimly, heading into the hotel with Red. He pointed back to where Roy was getting out of the cab.

"No autographs." Roy ducked past the man.

"Jesus God, Roy," he cried in a broken voice. He caught Roy's arm and held on to it. "Don't pass me by, for the love of God."

"What d'you want?" Roy stared, suspicious.

"Roy, you don't know me," the man sobbed. "My name's Mike Barney and I drive a truck for Cudahy's. I don't want a thing for myself, only a favor for my boy Pete. He was hurt in an accident, playin' in the street. They operated him for a broken skull a coupla days ago and he ain't doin' so good. The doctor says he ain't fightin' much."

Mike Barney's mouth twisted and he wept.

"What has that got to do with me?" Roy asked, white-faced.

The truck driver wiped his eyes on his sleeve. "Pete's a fan of yours, Roy. He got a scrapbook that thick fulla pictures of you. Yesterday they lemme go in and see him and I said to Pete you told me you'd sock a homer for him in the game tonight. After that he sorta smiled and looked better. They gonna let him listen a little tonight, and I know if you will hit one it will save him."

"Why did you say that for?" Roy said bitterly. "The way I am now I couldn't hit the side of a barn."

Holding to Roy's sleeve, Mike Barney fell to his knees. "Please, you gotta do it."

"Get up," Roy said. He pitied the guy and wanted to help him yet was afraid what would happen if he couldn't. He didn't want that responsibility.

Mike Barney stayed on his knees, sobbing. A crowd had collected and was watching them.

"I will do the best I can if I get the chance." Roy wrenched his sleeve free and hurried into the lobby.

"A father's blessing on you," the truck driver called after him in a cracked voice.

Dressing in the visitors' clubhouse for the game that night, Roy thought about the kid in the hospital. He had been thinking of him on and off and was anxious to do something for him. He could see himself walking up to the plate and clobbering a long one into the stands and then he imagined the boy, healed and whole, thanking him for saving his life. The picture was unusually vivid, and as he polished Wonderboy, his fingers itched to carry it into the batter's box and let go at a fat one.

But Pop had other plans. "You are still on the bench, Roy, unless you put that Wonderboy away and use a different stick."

Roy shook his head and Pop gave the line-up card to the ump without his name on it. When Mike Barney, sitting a few rows behind a box above third base, heard the announcement of the Knights' line-up without Roy in it, his face broke out in a sickish sweat.

The game began, Roy taking his non-playing position on the far corner of the bench and holding Wonderboy between his knees. It was a clear, warm night and the stands were just about full. The floods on the roof lit up the stadium brighter than day. Above the globe of light lay the dark night, and high in the sky the stars glittered. Though unhappy not to be playing, Roy, for no reason he could think of, felt better in his body than he had in a week. He had a hunch things could go well for him tonight, which was why he especially regretted not being in the game. Furthermore, Mike Barney was directly in his line of vision and sometimes stared at him. Roy's gaze went past him, farther down the stands, to where a young black-haired woman, wearing a red dress, was sitting at an aisle seat in short left. He could clearly see the white flower she wore pinned on her bosom and that she seemed to spend more time craning to get a look into the Knights' dugout—at him, he could swear—than in watching the game. She interested him, in that red dress, and he would have liked a close gander at her but he couldn't get out there without arousing attention.

Pop was pitching Fowler, who had kept going pretty well during the two dismal weeks of Roy's slump, only he was very crabby at everybody—especially Roy—for not getting him any runs, and causing him to lose two well-pitched games. As a result Pop had to keep after him in the late innings, because when Fowler felt disgusted he wouldn't bear down on the opposing batters.

Up through the fifth he had kept the Cubs bottled up but he eased off the next inning and they reached him for two runs with only one out. Pop gave him a fierce glaring at and Fowler then tightened and finished off the side with a pop fly and strikeout. In the Knights' half of the seventh, Cal Baker came through with a stinging triple, scoring Stubbs, and was himself driven in by Flores' single. That tied the score but it became untied when, in their part of the inning, the Cubs placed two doubles back to back, to produce another run.

As the game went on Roy grew tense. He considered telling Pop about the kid and asking for a chance to hit. But Pop was a stubborn cuss and Roy knew he'd continue to insist on him laying Wonderboy aside. This he was afraid to do. Much as he wanted to help the boy—and it really troubled him now—he felt he didn't stand a Chinaman's chance at a hit without his own club. And if he once abandoned Wonderboy there was no telling what would happen to him. Probably it would finish his career for keeps, because never since he had made the bat had he swung at a ball with any other.

In the eighth on a double and sacrifice, Pop worked a runner around to third. The squeeze failed so he looked around anxiously for a pinch hitter. Catching Roy's eye, he said, as Roy had thought he would, "Take a decent stick and go on up there."

Roy didn't move. He was sweating heavily and it cost him a great effort to stay put. He could see the truck driver suffering in his seat, wiping his face, cracking his knuckles, and sighing. Roy averted his glance.

There was a commotion in the lower left field stands. This lady in the red dress, whoever she was, had risen, and standing in a sea of gaping faces, seemed to be searching for someone. Then she looked toward the Knights' dugout and sort of half bowed her head. A murmur went up from the crowd. Some of them explained it that she had got mixed up about the seventh inning stretch and others answered how could she when the scoreboard showed the seventh inning was over? As she stood there, so cleanly etched in light, as if trying to communicate something she couldn't express, some of the fans were embarrassed. And the stranger sitting next to her felt a strong sexual urge which he concealed behind an impatient cigarette. Roy scarcely noticed her because he was lost in worry, seriously considering whether he ought to give up on Wonderboy.

Pop of course had no idea what was going on in Roy's head, so he gave the nod to Ed Simmons, a substitute infielder. Ed picked a bat out of the rack and as he approached the plate the standing lady slowly sat down. Everyone seemed to forget her then. Ed flied out. Pop looked scornfully at Roy and shot a stream of snuff into the dust.

Fowler had a little more trouble in the Cubs' half of the eighth but a double play saved him, and the score was still 3–2. The ninth opened. Pop appeared worn out. Roy had his eyes shut. It was Fowler's turn to bat. The second guessers were certain Pop would yank him for a pinch hitter but Fowler was a pretty fair hitter for a pitcher, and if the Knights could tie the score, his pitching tonight was too good to waste. He swung at the first ball, connecting for a line drive single, to Pop's satisfaction. Allie Stubbs tried to lay one away but his hard-hit fly ball to center was caught. To everybody's surprise Fowler went down the white line on the next pitch and dove safe into second under a cloud of dust. A long single could tie the score, but Cal Baker, to his disgust, struck out and flung his bat away. Pop again searched the bench for a pinch hitter. He fastened his gaze on Roy but Roy was unapproachable. Pop turned bitterly away.

Mike Barney, a picture of despair, was doing exercises of grief. He stretched forth his long hairy arms, his knobby hands clasped, pleading. Roy felt as though they were reaching right into the dugout to throttle him.

He couldn't stand it any longer. "I give up." Placing Wonderboy on the bench he rose and stood abjectly in front of Pop.

Pop looked up at him sadly. "You win," he said. "Go on in."

Roy gulped. "With my own bat?"

Pop nodded and gazed away.

Roy got Wonderboy and walked out into the light. A roar of recognition drowned the announcement of his name but not the loud beating of his heart. Though he'd been at bat only three days ago, it felt like years—an ageless time. He almost wept at how long it had been.

Lon Toomey, the hulking Cub hurler, who had twice in the last two weeks handed Roy his lumps, smiled behind his glove. He shot a quick glance at Fowler on second, fingered the ball, reared and threw. Roy, at the plate, watched it streak by.

"Stuh-rike."

He toed in, his fears returning. What if the slump did not give way? How much longer could it go on without destroying him?

Toomey lifted his right leg high and threw. Roy swung from his heels at a bad ball and the umpire sneezed in the breeze.

"Strike two!"

Wonderboy resembled a sagging baloney. Pop cursed the bat and some of the Knights' rooters among the fans booed. Mike Barney's harrowed puss looked yellow.

Roy felt sick with remorse that he hadn't laid aside Wonderboy in the beginning and gone into the game with four licks at bat instead of only three miserable strikes, two of which he already used up. How could he explain to Barney that he had traded his kid's life away out of loyalty to a hunk of wood?

The lady in the stands hesitantly rose for the second time. A photographer who had stationed himself nearby snapped a clear shot of her. She was an attractive woman, around thirty, maybe more, and built solid but not too big. Her bosom was neat, and her dark hair, parted on the side, hung loose and soft. A reporter approached her and asked her name but she wouldn't give it to him, nor would she, blushing, say why she was standing now. The fans behind her hooted, "Down in front," but though her eyes showed she was troubled she remained standing.

Noticing Toomey watching her, Roy stole a quick look. He caught the red dress and a white rose, turned away, then came quickly back for another take, drawn by the feeling that her smile was for him. Now why would she do that for? She seemed to be wanting to say something, and then it flashed on him the reason she was standing was to show her confidence in him. He felt surprised that anybody would want to do that for him. At the same time he became aware that the night had spread out in all directions and was filled with an unbelievable fragrance.

A pitch streaked toward him. Toomey had pulled a fast one. With a sob Roy fell back and swung.

Part of the crowd broke for the exits. Mike Barney wept freely now, and the lady who had stood up for Roy absently pulled on her white gloves and left.

The ball shot though Toomey's astounded legs and began to climb. The second baseman, laying back on the grass on a hunch, stabbed high for it but it leaped over his straining fingers, sailed through the light and up into the dark, like a white star seeking an old constellation.

Toomey, shrunk to a pygmy, stared into the vast sky.

Roy circled the bases like a Mississippi steamboat, lights lit, flags fluttering, whistle banging, coming round the bend. The Knights poured out of their dugout to pound his back, and hundreds of their rooters hopped about in the field. He stood on the home base, lifting his cap to the lady's empty seat.

And though Fowler goose-egged the Cubs in the last of the ninth and got credit for the win, everybody knew it was Roy alone who had saved the boy's life.

There Used to Be a Ballpark

BY JOE RAPOSO

And there used to be a ballpark
where the field was warm and green,
and the people played their crazy game
with a joy I'd never seen.
And the air was such a wonder
from the hot dogs and the beer,
yes, there used to be a ballpark right here.

And there used to be rock candy
and a big Fourth of July
with the fireworks exploding
all across the summer sky.
And the people watched in wonder;
how they'd laugh and how they'd cheer,
and there used to be a ballpark right here.

Now the children try to find it
and they can't believe their eyes,
'cause the old team isn't playing
and the new team hardly tries.
And the sky has got so cloudy
when it used to be so clear,
and the summer went so quickly this year.

Yes, there used to be a ballpark right here.

BASEBALL IS RELIGION WITHOUT THE MISCHIEF.

—THOMAS BOSWELL

Konjo, Wa, & Doryoku:
Baseball in Japan

☆ Japan has been playing forms of baseball since 1873, when it began there as a club sport. The first team was the Shinbashi Athletic Club Athletics. In 1896, the Ichiko team defeated a team of American traders and missionaries, starting the craze that made baseball the new Japanese national sport.

☆ The first Japanese superstar was pitcher Tsunetaro Moriyama at the turn of the 20th century. Legend has it that in his daily practice, he threw a ball at a brick wall until he wore a hole in it. This practice permanently bent his arm.

☆ There are currently 12 teams in Japanese professional baseball. They are divided into two six-team leagues: the Central League and the Pacific League, which includes the Hanshin Tigers, the Yomiuri Giants, and the Hiroshima Toyo Carp.

☆ The first professional team in Japan, the Giants, had to undergo a hard preseason training. This included the "Thousand Fungo Drill," in which young players had to dive for ground balls until they collapsed from exhaustion.

☆ Japanese players don't just practice on the field; they are also required to attend nightly classroom sessions to review plays and strategies.

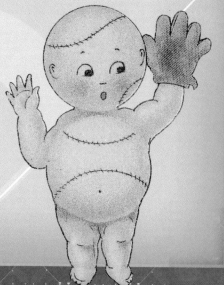

- Going to a baseball game in Japan is a completely new experience for the average American fan. There are often bands that play Beethoven in opening ceremonies, umpires who practice their calls during the pregame warm-up, and commentators who will announce a player's blood type—a fact believed to affect performance.

- There are two types of fans at a Japanese ballpark: individual fans, and those who are part of an *oedan*, or organized cheering group. The individual sits quietly as the game goes on, returning foul balls to umpires and avoiding vulgar displays. The *oedan*, on the other hand, show up early to games to practice cheers; bring whistles, drums, and horns to the stadium; and follow their captain to keep up a constant display of noise and energy.

- Japanese ballplayers value proper form, rote learning, and harmony over aggressiveness and individual accomplishment.

- Sacrificing for your team is considered an honor in Japan. A fine example of this came in 2003, when Giants infielder Masahiro Kawai broke the record for career sacrifice bunts with a total of 514. There was a huge celebration that night, including fireworks over the Tokyo Dome and a ceremony featuring Kawai's wife and children.

- Three terms best describe Japanese baseball: *konjo* (fighting spirit), *wa* (group harmony), and *doryoku* (effort). Two famous players, Sadaharu Oh and Koji Yamamoto, even sign their autograph with the character for *doryoku*.

- Rules are plentiful for Japanese teams. Some have bans on drinking, smoking, and appearing in commercials. During the game, there can be no throwing of gloves or bats or screaming on the field. Respecting the manager is also of the utmost importance, and some teams strictly enforce diets, showers, and curfews.

Cincinnati Reds' Chili

1 lb. ground round

2 yellow onions, diced

1 small bottle of ketchup

2 cans of tomatoes
(14.5 ounces each)
or 4 cups diced and
stewed tomatoes

1 teaspoon cayenne
pepper (or more if
you like it spicy)

1 teaspoon chili powder
(or more if you like
it spicy)

1 ground allspice

$\frac{1}{2}$ teaspoon cinnamon

1 teaspoon
unsweetened cocoa

$\frac{1}{2}$ cup water

1 cup grated
cheddar cheese

salt and pepper to taste

Did you know that Cincinnati has the highest number of chili joints per capita in the country? So its no wonder that fans of the Reds also enjoy the game with Chili—their way—on top of a hot dog or spaghetti. So the next time you have leftover pasta or hot dogs from a backyard get-together, whip up some chili to enjoy it all while you catch the game!

1. Cook the meat over a medium-high heat, stirring until the meat is brown, crumbled, and cooked through.

2. Add the onions and water and bring to a boil.

3. Add the rest of the ingredients and simmer for 1 $\frac{1}{2}$ hours.

4. Remove from heat. Add salt and pepper to taste.

5. Add to spaghetti or hot dogs and sprinkle with grated cheese.

Serves 6

THE ONE CONSTANT THROUGH ALL
THE YEARS HAS BEEN BASEBALL.
AMERICA HAS ROLLED BY LIKE
AN ARMY OF STEAMROLLERS.
IT'S BEEN ERASED LIKE A
BLACKBOARD, REBUILT, AND
ERASED AGAIN. BUT BASEBALL
HAS MARKED THE TIME. THIS
FIELD, THIS GAME, IS A PART OF
OUR PAST. IT REMINDS US OF ALL
THAT ONCE WAS GOOD, AND WHAT
COULD BE AGAIN.

—JAMES EARL JONES IN *Field of Dreams*

FROM
BULL DURHAM
BY RON SHELTON

I believe in the Church of Baseball. I've tried all the major religions, and most of the minor ones. I've worshipped Buddha, Allah, Brahma, Vishnu, Siva, trees, mushrooms, and Isadora Duncan. I know things. For instance, there are 108 beads in a Catholic rosary and there are 108 stitches in a baseball. When I heard that, I gave Jesus a chance. But it just didn't work out between us. The Lord laid too much guilt on me. I prefer metaphysics to theology. You see, there's no guilt in baseball, and it's never boring.... I've tried 'em all, I really have, and the only church that truly feeds the soul, day in, day out, is the Church of Baseball.

BASEBALL
ON THE BIG SCREEN

☆ *Bull Durham* (1988) COMEDY/ROMANCE
A comic love triangle is formed among a fan who sleeps with one minor-league baseball player each season, a rising but immature pitcher, and the cynical older player brought in to mature him.

☆ *Field of Dreams* (1989) DRAMA
An Iowa farmer hears voices that guide him to build a baseball field. Along with a reclusive author, he embarks on a journey that will culminate with the ghosts of Shoeless Joe and seven other 1919 White Sox team members playing under the lights of his field.

☆ *Eight Men Out* (1988) DRAMA
A true story, based on the 1919 World Series. Due to a labor dispute with their wealthy manager, eight White Sox players decide to throw the Series for money and are banished from baseball for life.

☆ *The Pride of the Yankees* (1942) DRAMA
A biopic that follows the life of baseball great Lou Gehrig, who played 2,130

straight games before being forced to retire due to a nerve disease.

☆ *The Bad News Bears* (1976) COMEDY
A team of misfits is coached by a former minor leaguer in California's competitive Little League baseball. All seems lost until a few unexpected additions are made to the roster and the Bears rise to the challenge of beating their rivals. The film was remade in 2005.

☆ *The Natural* (1984) DRAMA
An older player comes out of nowhere to lead his '30s team to the top. Armed with an almost magical natural ability for the game and a bat made from a tree once struck by lightning, his passion for the game inspires everyone around him.

☆ *A League of Their Own* (1992) COMEDY/DRAMA
A story of two sisters who join the All-American Girls Professional Baseball League during World War II, when the men's teams are being emptied by the draft. The sisters and their teammates struggle to balance their lives as professional athletes and their lives as women in the '40s.

☆ *The Sandlot* (1993) COMEDY/FAMILY
A boy moves into a new neighborhood and becomes part of a group of friends who spend their summer playing baseball, flirting with the older lifeguard at the pool, and avoiding the evil dog behind the fence of their field.

☆ *Major League* (1989) COMEDY
When the Cleveland Indians—on a record-setting losing streak—realize that their new owner is trying to move them to a warmer climate by assembling the worst team ever, the group of misfits attempts to foil her plan by rallying for the division title.

☆ *It Happens Every Spring* (1949) COMEDY
A professor accidentally develops a fluid that is repelled by wood. With his new discovery, he becomes the pitcher for St. Louis and leads them to the World Series.

☆ *The Stratton Story* (1949) DRAMA
A true story about the winning White Sox pitcher Monty Stratton, who loses a leg to amputation three years into his major league baseball career. With the support of his wife and a wooden leg, he returns to the minor leagues and plays for several more years.

☆ *Bang the Drum Slowly* (1973) DRAMA
A star pitcher for a New York team learns his catcher has a terminal illness. The catcher, an average player with a big heart, is supported by his friendship with the pitcher in what he knows will be his last season.

☆ *The Rookie* (2002) FAMILY
A talented but injured minor-league player gives up his dream and becomes a high school baseball coach. Twelve years later, his team makes a deal with him: If they make it to the state tournament, he has to try out for a major-league team.

☆ *Angels in the Outfield* (1994) FAMILY
A young boy wants his family back together, but his father says it will only happen if his favorite baseball team wins the pennant. The team is currently

in last place but is aided by the boy's prayers and a few angels only he can see.

☆ *Damn Yankees!* (1958) MUSICAL
Adapted from the musical about a Washington Senators fan who makes a deal with the devil in exchange for his team winning the pennant.

☆ *Baseball: A Film by Ken Burns* (1994) PBS DOCUMENTARY
More than 18 hours long, this documentary suggests that baseball is the game that defines America. Divided into nine innings, it features the sport's most important moments as well as the social issues that have surrounded it.

☆ *Alibi Ike* (1935) COMEDY
A great baseball player who always has an excuse for everything loses his girlfriend because of it, and gets pressured by gamblers to throw the World Series.

☆ *61** (2001) HBO DRAMA
The story of Yankees Mickey Mantle and Roger Maris during the summer of 1961, when they chased Babe's home run record.

☆ *Kill the Umpire* (1950) COMEDY
A player is forced to become an umpire against his will, and learns how difficult it is for the man calling the strikes.

☆ *The Babe* (1992) FAMILY
The baseball legend goes from orphanage to superstardom he becomes an inspiration to young children—even though he possesses some unflattering habits.

☆ *The Bingo Long Traveling All-Stars & Motor Kings* (1976) COMEDY
Negro League players rebel when a bad owner refuses to allow Negro League players to play other black teams, so they start their own team. They make money by playing all-white teams as a traveling show.

☆ *The Jackie Robinson Story* (1950) DRAMA
Jackie plays himself in the story of his life, showing the difficulties of rising above the racial tensions during his landmark career.

A HOT DOG AT THE BALLPARK IS BETTER THAN STEAK AT THE RITZ.

—HUMPHREY BOGART

The Brewers' Brats

8 bratwurst

Beer, to cover
(use your favorite lager)

1 onion, chopped

¼ cup (½ stick) butter

Visiting Milwaukee during baseball season is quite an affair. You can watch Bernie the Brewer and the racing sausages, see the statue of Hank Aaron, and, most importantly, sample one of the famous bratwurst. Our recipe adds the perfect midwestern touch, marinating the brats in beer before grilling.

1. Marinate the brats in a mixture of the beer and onion for a few hours before cooking (overnight, if possible).

2. Place the brats on a plate and transfer the marinade into a pan. Bring to a boil.

3. Add the butter and stir until melted. Reduce to a simmer; add the brats and simmer 30 minutes or until cooked.

4. Transfer to the grill and grill to satisfaction.

5. Serve on a bun with ketchup, mustard, and onions or sauerkraut.

Makes 8 brats.

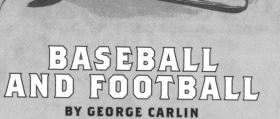

BASEBALL AND FOOTBALL

BY GEORGE CARLIN

Baseball is different from any other sport; very different. For instance, in most sports you score points or goals, in baseball you score runs.

In most sports the ball, or object, is put in play by the offensive team; in baseball the defensive team puts the ball in play, and only the defense is allowed to touch the ball. In fact, in baseball if an offensive player touches the ball intentionally, he's out; sometimes unintentionally, he's out.

Also: In football, basketball, soccer, volleyball, and all sports played with a ball, you score *with* the ball, and without the ball you can't score. In baseball the ball prevents you from scoring.

In most sports the team is run by a coach; in baseball the team is run by a manager; and only in baseball does the manager (or coach) wear the same clothing the players do. If you had ever seen John Madden in his Oakland Raiders football uniform, you would know the reason for this custom.

Now, I've mentioned football. Baseball and football are the two most popular spectator sports in this country. And, as such, it seems they ought to be able to tell us something about ourselves and our values. And maybe how those values have changed over the last 150 years. For those reasons, I enjoy comparing baseball and football:

Baseball is a nineteenth-century pastoral game.
Football is a twentieth-century technological struggle.

Baseball is played on a diamond, in a park. The baseball park!
Football is played on a gridiron, in a stadium, sometimes called
   Soldier Field or War Memorial Stadium.

Baseball begins in the spring, the season of new life.
Football begins in the fall, when everything is dying.

In football you wear a helmet.
In baseball you wear a cap.

Football is concerned with *downs*. "What down is it?"
Baseball is concerned with *ups*. "Who's up? Are you up? I'm not up!
   He's up!"

In football you receive a penalty.
In baseball you make an error.

243

In football the specialist comes in to kick.
In baseball the specialist comes in to relieve somebody.

Football has hitting, clipping, spearing, piling on, personal fouls, late
hitting, and unnecessary roughness.
Baseball has the sacrifice.

Football is played in any kind of weather: Rain, snow, sleet,
hail, fog . . . can't see the game, don't know if
there is a game going on; mud on the
field . . . can't read the uniforms,
can't read the yard markers, the
struggle will continue!
In baseball if it rains, we don't
go out to play. "I can't go out! It's raining out!"

Baseball has the seventh-inning stretch.
Football has the two-minute warning.

Baseball has no time limit: "We don't know when it's
gonna end!"
Football is rigidly timed, and it will end "even if we
have to go to sudden death."

244

In baseball, during the game, in the stands, there's a kind of picnic feeling. Emotions may run high or low, but there's not that much unpleasantness.

In football, during the game in the stands, you can be sure that at least twenty-seven times you were perfectly capable of taking the life of a fellow human being.

And finally, the objectives of the two games are completely different:

In football the object is for the quarterback, otherwise known as the field general, to be on target with his aerial assault, riddling the defense by hitting his receivers with deadly accuracy in spite of the blitz, even if he has to use the shotgun. With short bullet passes and long bombs, he marches his troops into enemy territory, balancing this aerial assault with a sustained ground attack that punches holes in the forward wall of the enemy's defensive line.

In baseball the object is to go home! And to be safe! "I hope I'll be safe at home!"

IF A WOMAN HAS TO CHOOSE BETWEEN CATCHING A FLY BALL AND SAVING AN INFANT'S LIFE, SHE WILL CHOOSE TO SAVE THE INFANT'S LIFE WITHOUT EVEN CONSIDERING IF THERE IS A MAN ON BASE.

—DAVE BARRY

Instruction

Conrad Hilberry

The coach has taught her how to swing,

run bases, slide, how to throw

to second, flip off her mask for fouls.

Now, on her own, she studies

how to knock the dirt out of her cleats,

hitch up her pants, miss her shoulder

with a stream of spit, bump

her fist into her catcher's mitt,

and stare incredulously at the ump.

248

WHEN WORLD WAR II STARTED, women stepped up to bat for their country. Most did so by working in factories or planting Victory Gardens, but a few had the rare opportunity to lend a hand with a ball and glove. The All-American Girls Professional Baseball League provided a country at war with entertainment

ALL-AMERICAN GIRLS

and inspiration, as well as ensuring the preservation of America's favorite pastime.

Philip K. Wrigley, owner of the Chicago Cubs, watched as major-league ballplayers were drafted into the war. He worried about the fate of baseball and its grand stadiums while the star players were overseas. In response, he formed a committee to brainstorm ideas to maintain the business of baseball. Their solution was to form a women's league.

Major-league scouts traveled across the country in order to find the best players for spring-training tryouts. On May 17, 1943, 280 hopefuls filled Wrigley Field. The standards for the players were high. Not only were they required to be excellent hitters, runners, and sliders, but they also had to embody the image of the American girl. Helena Rubenstein's Beauty Salon worked with the girls to develop strict hygiene practices that included "Morning and Night" and "After the Game" rituals. There were rules regarding hair length (no bobs), when to wear lipstick (always), and when to attend social engagements without a chaperone (never). It was felt that the players would have a lot of responsibility representing the league in a proper manner.

When the final rosters were posted, the new members of the AAGPBL were ready. Armed with new uniforms, beauty kits, and salaries of $45 to $85 a week, the players reported to their new teams in Racine, Kenosha, Rockford, and South Bend. Among them were a wide range of athletes, from Dottie Schoeder, a 15-year-old from a small farm in Illinois, to the seasoned softball star Anne Harnett.

The first season in 1943 was a trial. The girls had to adapt to a new hybrid of the game. In order to entice fans, the league combined girls' softball with crowd-pleasing elements of baseball such as longer pitches and base stealing. In the end, the season was rated a success, with attendance totaling 176,612. The Racine Belles won the World Championship, and Americans got behind their baseball-playing girls.

The on-field contributions were not the only thing that made the league so remarkable. The teams played exhibition games to support the Red Cross and visited wounded veterans in army hospitals. At the start of each game, the teams formed a V for victory and sang "The Star Spangled Banner." With each show of patriotism and skill, the league gained fans. In the second season, two new franchises joined and attendance continued to rise. By 1946, 10,000 fans were in attendance for a Fourth of July doubleheader in South Bend.

When the war ended and television started broadcasting major-league games, interest in the AAGPBL drifted away; the last season took place in 1954. But thanks to the league, more than 600 women were given the opportunity to play at a competitive level, and a country at war had a brand-new image of "All-American Girls" to rally around.

PROGRESS ALWAYS INVOLVES RISKS. YOU CAN'T STEAL SECOND BASE AND KEEP YOUR FOOT ON FIRST.

—FREDERICK B. WILCOX

Richmond Stadium, Richmond, Virginia

Fenway Park, Boston, Massachusetts

THE GREEN FIELDS OF THE MIND

BY A. BARTLETT GIAMATTI

It breaks your heart. It is designed to break your heart. The game begins in the spring, when everything else begins again, and it blossoms in the summer, filling the afternoons and evenings, and then as soon as the chill rains come, it stops and leaves you to face the fall alone. You count on it, rely on it to buffer the passage of time, to keep the memory of sunshine and high skies alive, and then just when the days are all twilight, when you need it most, it stops. Today, October 2, a Sunday of rain and broken branches and leaf-clogged drains and slick streets, it stopped, and summer was gone.

Somehow, the summer seemed to slip by faster this time. Maybe it wasn't this summer, but all the summers that, in this my fortieth summer, slipped by so fast. There comes a time when every summer will have something of autumn about it. Whatever the reason, it seemed to me that I was investing more and more in baseball, making the game do more of the work that keeps time fat and slow and lazy. I was counting on the game's deep patterns, three strikes, three outs, three times three innings, and its deepest impulse, to go out and back, to leave and to return home, to set the order of the day and to organize the daylight. I wrote a few things this last summer, this summer that did not last, nothing grand but some things, and yet that work was just camouflage. The real activity was done with the radio—not the all-seeing, all-falsifying television—and was the playing of the game in the only place it will last, the enclosed, green field of the mind. There, in that warm, bright place, what the old poet called Mutability does not so quickly come.

But out here on Sunday, October 2, where it rains all day, Dame Mutability never loses. She was in the crowd at Fenway yesterday, a gray day full of bluster and contradiction, when the Red Sox came up in the last of the ninth trailing Baltimore 8–5, while the Yankees, rain-delayed against Detroit, only needing to win one or have Boston lose one to win it all, sat in New York washing down cold cuts with beer and watching the Boston game. Boston had won two, the Yankees had lost two, and suddenly it seemed as if the whole season might go to the last day, or beyond, except here was Boston losing 8–5, while New York sat in its family room and put its feet up. Lynn, both ankles hurting now as they had in July, hits a single down the right-field line. The crowd stirs. It is on its feet. Hobson, third baseman, former Bear Bryant quarterback, strong, quiet, over 100 RBIs, goes for three breaking balls and is out. The goddess smiles and encourages her agent, a canny journeyman named Nelson Briles.

Now comes a pinch hitter, Bernie Carbo, one-time Rookie of the Year, erratic, quick, a shade too handsome, so laid back he is always, in his soul, stretched out in the tall grass, one arm under his head, watching the clouds and laughing; now he looks over some low stuff unworthy of him and then, uncoiling, sends one out, straight on a right line, over the center-field wall, no cheap Fenway shot, but all of it, the physics as elegant as the arc the ball describes.

New England is on its feet, roaring. The summer will not pass. Roaring, they recall the evening, late and cold, in 1975, the sixth game of the World Series, perhaps the greatest baseball game played in the last fifty years, when Carbo, loose and easy, had uncoiled to tie the game that Fisk would win. It is 8–7, one out, and school will never start, rain will never come, sun will warm the back of your neck forever. Now Bailey, picked up from the National League recently, big arms, heavy gut, experienced, new to the league and the club; he fouls off two and then, checking, tentative, a big man off balance, he pops a soft liner to the first baseman. It is suddenly darker and later, and the announcer doing the game coast to coast, a New Yorker who works for a New York television station, sounds relieved. His little world, well-lit, hot-combed, split-second-timed, had no capacity to absorb this much gritty, grainy, contrary reality.

Cox swings a bat, stretches his long arms, bends his back, the rookie from Pawtucket, who broke in two weeks earlier with a record six straight hits, the kid drafted ahead of Fred Lynn, rangy, smooth, cool. The count runs two-and-two, Briles is cagey, nothing too good, and Cox swings, the ball beginning toward the mound and then, in a jaunty, wayward dance, skipping past Briles, feinting to the right, skimming the last of the grass, finding the dirt, moving now like some small, purposeful marine creature negotiating the green deep, easily avoiding the jagged rock of second base, traveling steady and straight now out into the dark, silent recesses of center field.

The aisles are jammed, the place is on its feet, the wrappers, the programs, the Coke cups and peanut shells, the detritus of an afternoon; the anxieties, the things that have to be done tomorrow, the regrets about yesterday, the accumulation of a summer: all forgotten, while hope, the anchor, bites and takes hold where a moment before it seemed we would be swept out with the tide. Rice is up, Rice whom Aaron had said was the only one he'd seen with the ability to break his records, Rice the best clutch hitter on the club, with the best slugging percentage in the league, Rice, so quick and strong he once checked his swing halfway through and snapped the bat in two, Rice the Hammer of God sent to scourge the Yankees, the sound was overwhelming, fathers pounded their sons on the back, cars pulled off the road, households froze, New England exulted in its blessedness and roared its thanks for all good things, for Rice and for a summer stretching halfway through October. Briles threw, Rice swung, and it was over. One pitch, a fly to center, and it stopped. Summer died in New England and like rain sliding off a roof, the crowd slipped out of Fenway, quickly, with only a steady murmur of concern for the drive ahead remaining of the roar. Mutability had turned the seasons and translated hope to memory once again. And once again, she had used baseball, our best invention to stay change, to bring change on. That is why it breaks my heart, that game—not because in New York they could win because Boston lost; in that, there is a rough justice, and a reminder to the Yankees of how slight and fragile are the circumstances that exalt one group of human beings over another. It breaks my heart because it was meant to foster in me again the illusion that there was something abiding, some pattern and some impulse that could come together to make a reality that would resist the corrosion; and because after it had fostered again that most hungered-for illusion, the game was meant to stop, and betray precisely what it promised.

Of course, there are those who learn after the first few times. They grow out of sports. And there are others who were born with the wisdom to know that nothing lasts. These are the truly tough among us, the ones who can live without illusion, or without even the hope of illusion. I am not that grown-up or up-to-date. I am a simpler creature, tied to more primitive patterns and cycles. I need to think something lasts forever, and it might as well be that state of being that is a game; it might as well be that, in a green field, in the sun.

OPENING DAY

U.S. presidents have thrown out the first pitch on Opening Day, including the impressive Harry Truman, who threw one with his left and one with his right hand.

☆ Since 1903, 33 teams have lost their opener and still won the World Series.

☆ Stadiums often celebrate Opening Day with interesting promotions, but no other team can hold a candle to the Philadelphia Phillies. Characters who have shown up at their first games include a man who parachuted onto the field, another who hang-glided above the stadium, one with a rocket strapped to his back, and an acrobat who did stunts hanging from a helicopter.

☆ As Major League Baseball's first officially recognized team, the Cincinnati Reds were given the honor of hosting the first game on Opening Day in every season from 1876 to 1989.

☆ William Taft was the first president to attend an Opening Day, at a Washington Nationals game in 1910. Since then, 11

☆ In 1946, the Boston Braves painted a new coat of red on the stadium seats, but the cold weather didn't allow it to dry before the game. Hundreds of fans left the game angry, and the Braves were forced to pick up everyone's dry-cleaning bill.

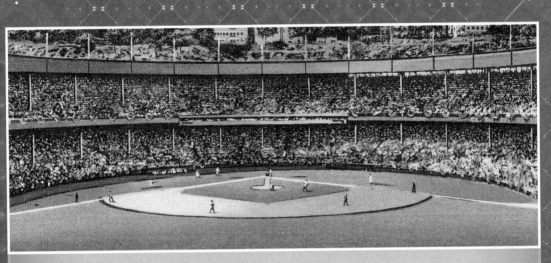

☆ Opening Day 1946 was a thirsty one for fans at the new Dodger Stadium. As the game began, officials realized the architects had forgotten to include drinking fountains.

☆ Babe Ruth christened the new Yankee Stadium in 1923 with a three-run homer. In 1929, he hit another Opening Day homer in honor of the woman he'd married the day before.

☆ The only man to hit for the cycle on Opening Day was Gee Walker of the Tigers in 1937.

☆ In April 1974, Hank Aaron started the season with his 714th career home run at his first at-bat, tying Babe Ruth's record.

☆ Throughout the season, boldfaced entries on team rosters are the players who started on Opening Day.

☆ "Commencement of the Season" is how Alexander Cartwright described Opening Day on his scoresheet for the first Knickerbocker Club of New York game, April 10, 1846.

☆ There has been only one no-hitter thrown on Opening Day, by Cleveland's Bob Feller in 1940. It was only 35 degrees at Chicago's Comiskey Park during that game.

NO MATTER WHAT I TALK ABOUT, I ALWAYS GET BACK TO BASEBALL.

—CONNIE MACK

Texas Rangers' Fajita Enchiladas

This recipe is straight from the experts at the Texas Rangers' Ameriquest Field. The chefs' in Arlington keep fans happy with these tasty fajitas that are full of flavor. With garlic, lime juice, peppers, and guacamole, they make the perfect ballgame meal.

1. In a large bowl, whisk together garlic, lime juice, cumin and oil.

2. Add steak to the marinade, turning it to coat it well. Cover, chill for at least one hour or overnight—the longer the better.

3. Grill steak 3 to 4 minutes on each side (medium rare).

4. Let meat stand for about 5 minutes on cutting board and then cut into thin strips across the grain.

5. In large skillet, heat oil over moderate heat until hot but not smoking. Add onions and cook for 1 minute, then add peppers, season with salt and pepper, and sauté for 5 more minutes or until peppers are soft. Add beef to pan, stir and remove from heat.

6. Lay each large tortilla flat and place half of the beef mixture along the center, and roll to close. Place tortillas side by side and cover with Queso cheese sauce and guacamole. Serve with salsa on side. This dish goes well with Spanish rice and refried beans.

Serves 2.

FOR MARINADE:

4 cloves chopped garlic

¼ cup fresh lime juice

1 ½ tablespoon ground cumin

2 tablespoons vegetable oil

2 lbs. skirt steak, trimmed and cut into large pieces to fit on grill

2 tablespoons vegetable oil

3 bell assorted peppers, sliced thin

1 large yellow or white onion, sliced thin

2 large flour tortillas

salt & pepper to taste

AS ACCOMPANIMENTS:

Queso cheese sauce

guacamole

fresh salsa

269

HELLO AGAIN, EVERYBODY.
IT'S A BEE-YOOO-TIFUL
DAY FOR BASEBALL.
—HARRY CARAY

FROM
THE INTERIOR STADIUM
BY ROGER ANGELL

Within the ballpark, time moves differently, marked by no clock except the events of the game. This is the unique, unchangeable feature of baseball and perhaps explains why this sport, for all the enormous changes it has undergone in the past decade or two, remains somehow rustic, unviolent, and introspective. Baseball's time is seamless and invisible, a bubble within which players move at exactly the same pace and rhythms as all their predecessors. This is the way the game was played in our youth and in our fathers' youth, and even back then—back in the country days—there must have been the same feeling that time could be stopped. Since baseball time is measured only in outs, all you have to do is succeed utterly; keep hitting, keep the rally alive, and you have defeated time. You remain forever young. Sitting in the stands, we sense this, if only dimly. The players below us—Mays, DiMaggio, Ruth, Snodgrass—swim and blur in memory, the ball floats over to Terry Turner, and the end of this game may never come.

Take Me Out to the Ball Game

Lyrics by Jack Norworth
Music by Albert von Tilzer

Katie Casey was baseball mad
Had the fever and had it bad
Just to root for the home town crew
Every sou Katie blew
On a Saturday her young beau
Called to see if she'd like to go
To see a show, but Miss Kate said, "No,
I'll tell you what you can do."

Take me out to the ball game
Take me out with the crowd.
Buy me some peanuts and Cracker Jack
I don't care if I never get back
Let me root, root, root for the home team
If they don't win, it's a shame
For it's one, two, three strikes, you're out
At the old ball game

Katie Casey saw all the games
Knew the players by their first names
Told the umpire he was wrong
All along, good and strong
When the score was just two to two
Katie Casey knew what to do
Just to cheer up the boys she knew
She made the gang sing this song

Not Just Peanuts & Cracker Jacks:
Stadium Fare

★ How did the hot dog get its name? Legend holds that it's a simple case of bad spelling. A newspaper cartoonist around 1906 was inspired to draw a strip based on the vendors at a baseball stadium, who yelled, "Get your red-hot dachshund sausages." He sketched a cartoon with a real dachshund dog, smeared with mustard in a bun, but because he couldn't spell the dog breed's name, he wrote, "Get your hot dogs"—and a new name was born.

★ An estimated 180 million hot dogs were eaten at baseball games in 2004. The fans at Dodger Stadium eat the most at 1.61 million, followed by Coors Field fans with 1.5 million, and Wrigley fans at 1.47 million. That's a lot of dogs!

★ The Dodgers are famous for their Dodger Dog: It's 12 inches long, weighs in at 76 grams, and, most importantly, is always grilled, never boiled.

★ The Fiesta Dog at Minute Maid Park is grilled and topped with red and green jalapeños.

- In Texas, they specialize in smoked brisket and turkey legs.

- In Philadelphia, the Phillie Phanatic mascot launches hot dogs into the stands, to the delight of young fans.

- Media entrepreneur Ted Turner raises the bison on his Montana ranch that supply meat for Turner Stadium's bison burgers and bison dogs.

- Though Cracker Jack was trademarked in 1896, it wasn't until 1912 that the treat began to include a toy in every box. Now the Cracker Jack company is the biggest user of small toys in the world!

- The name *Cracker Jack* comes from an old slang term that referred to something really great. As in, "Cracker Jack is really crackerjack! Don't ya think?"

- Denver's Coors Field offers stadiumgoers an in-house brewery featuring beers called Helles of A Play, Right Field Red, and Sandlot Game Time Decision Schwarzbier.

- U.S. Cellular Field in Chicago is famous for peanut butter and jelly sandwiches!

- Many stadiums, like the Bank One Ballpark (BOB) in Arizona, offer a Visiting Team Special. This consists of one menu item from the visiting team's home stadium as well as a beer from the visiting stadium.

- The Indians' Jacobs Field sells pretzels in the shape of the team's "I" logo.

- The San Diego Padres' PETCO Park serves a local favorite—Rubio's fish tacos.

- San Francisco's SBC Park has a varied menu including tofu hot dogs, tortellini, and a 40-clove garlic chicken sandwich.

Homemade Cracker Jack

1 cup
Spanish peanuts

1 cup (2 sticks) butter
or margarine

2 cups packed
brown sugar

1/2 cup
light corn syrup

1/2 teaspoon salt

1/2 teaspoon
baking soda

1 teaspoon
vanilla extract

6 cups popcorn

Continue the grand baseball tradition by serving up this great recipe at a party. Make sure everyone knows the old tune as well. That way, the next time they beg you to make this time-honored treat, they can do it with a smile and a song.

1. Preheat the oven to 250 degrees.

2. Mix the popcorn and peanuts in a large foil pan.

3. Melt the butter in a saucepan over medium heat. Add the brown sugar, corn syrup, and salt. Stir the mixture until it starts to boil, then boil for 5 minutes without stirring. Remove from the heat and stir in the soda and vanilla.

4. Pour over the popcorn and peanuts, stirring to coat. Bake, uncovered, 1 hour, stirring every 15 minutes.

5. Remove from the oven and spread out on waxed paper to cool. Break into pieces and serve.

Serves 6 to 8.

I'M NOT CONCERNED WITH YOUR LIKING OR DISLIKING ME. ALL I ASK IS THAT YOU RESPECT ME AS A HUMAN BEING.

—JACKIE ROBINSON

JACKIE ROBINSON

JACKIE ROBINSON STEPPED ONTO THE FIELD for the Brooklyn Dodgers in 1947—and changed the face of baseball forever. Born Jack Roosevelt Robinson on January 31, 1919, he was the grandson of a slave and son of a sharecropper. When his father left, Jackie's mother moved the family to California, where they were the only black family on his block. Early on, Jackie learned to depend on his family and his own drive to get by. He began to excel in sports at a young age and saw them as a way to succeed. All his athletic pursuits paid off when he attended UCLA as a four-letter athlete, the first person to do so in UCLA history. When financial difficulties forced Jackie to leave college for the army, he voiced his objections to the racial discrimination he experienced and was court-martialed. After being honorably discharged, Jackie was poised to make his break into professional athletics.

Signed by the Kansas City Monarchs, Jackie played one season in the Negro Leagues before he was approached in 1945 by the man who would alter his path forever. Branch Rickey, the president of the Brooklyn Dodgers, saw in Jackie a player who had the courage to stand up to segregation in baseball, and the strength to survive the pressure that would inevitably come.

With the support of his wife, Rachel, and his family, Jackie took on the challenge and proved to the world that he could play. At the end of his first season with the Dodgers, he won the Rookie of the Year Award, followed by the MVP Award two years later. But these acknowledgments did not mean the fight for respect was over for Robinson. Until then, he had kept quiet about the treatment on and off the field, some say due to a promise he had made to Rickey. After he was established in the league, however, Jackie begin to speak up when balls were thrown at his head, when fans yelled racial slurs, or when hate mail arrived at his door. On the field, the second baseman continued to be a threat with his high batting average and quickness on the base path—once stealing second, third, and home in a single inning. He was twice awarded the stolen base title, with his lifetime total capping off at 197. His contributions over 10 seasons led the Dodgers to six National League pennants and one World Series victory.

Jackie's retirement came in 1956, when he was told he was to be traded to the Giants. He chose to end his athletic career rather than play for the Dodgers' rivals. But with the end of one revolutionary career came the birth of many others for the pioneer. He became the vice president of the restaurant chain Chock Full o' Nuts, co-founded the Freedom National Bank of Harlem, and began the Jackie Robinson Construction Corporation, which built houses for low-income families. In all aspects of his life, Jackie made extraordinary efforts to advance the African American community.

In his first eligible year, 1962, Jackie Robinson was inducted into the Baseball Hall of Fame with his mother, wife, and Branch Rickey by his side. During a time of great unrest in America, Jackie once again was an inspiration to a community struggling to be recognized as equal. When he died in 1972, his pallbearers (including Pee Wee Reese, Larry Doby, Ralph Branca, and Junior Gilliam) spoke volumes for what he had done for the sport of baseball. Fifty years after he first broke the color barrier, Major League Baseball retired number 42 from all professional baseball, honoring his legacy for all time.

WHEN YOU COME TO A FORK IN THE ROAD, TAKE IT!

—YOGI BERRA

FROM

A CONNECTICUT YANKEE IN KING ARTHUR'S COURT

BY MARK TWAIN

At the end of the month I sent the vessel home for fresh supplies, and for news. We expected her back in three or four days. She would bring me, along with other news, the result of a certain experiment which I had been starting. It was a project of mine to replace the tournament with something which might furnish an escape for the extra steam of the chivalry, keep those bucks entertained and out of mischief, and at the same time preserve the best thing in them, which was their hardy spirit of emulation. I had had a choice band of them in private training for some time, and the date was now arriving for their first public effort.

This experiment was baseball. In order to give the thing vogue from the start, and place it out of the reach of criticism, I chose my nines by rank, not capacity. There wasn't a knight in either team who wasn't a sceptered sovereign. As for material of this sort, there was a glut of it always around Arthur. You couldn't throw a brick in any direction and not cripple a king. Of course, I couldn't get these people to leave off their armor; they wouldn't do that when they bathed. They consented to differentiate the armor so that a body could tell one team from the other, but that was the most they would do. So, one of the teams wore chain-mail ulsters, and the other wore plate armor made of my new Bessemer steel. Their practice in the field was the most fantastic thing I ever saw. Being ball-proof, they never skipped out of the way, but stood still and took the result; when a Bessemer was at the bat and a ball hit him, it would bound a hundred and fifty yards sometimes. And when a man was running, and threw himself on his stomach to slide to his base, it was like an iron-clad coming into port. At first I appointed men of no rank to act as umpires, but I had to discontinue that. These people were no easier to please than other nines. The umpire's first decision was usually his last; they broke him in two with a bat, and his friends toted him home on a shutter. When it was noticed that no umpire ever survived a game, umpiring got to be unpopular. So I was obliged to appoint somebody whose rank and lofty position under the government would protect him....

The first public game would certainly draw fifty thousand people; and for solid fun would be worth going around the world to see. Everything would be favorable; it was balmy and beautiful spring weather now, and Nature was all tailored out in her new clothes....

Baseball's Sad Lexicon

Franklin Pierce Adams

These are the saddest of possible words,

"Tinker to Evers to Chance."

Trio of Bear Cubs and fleeter than birds,

"Tinker to Evers to Chance."

Ruthlessly pricking our gonfalon bubble,

Making a Giant hit into a double,

Words that are weighty with nothing but trouble,

"Tinker to Evers to Chance."

293

Roberto Clemente

from World Series Dinner
Honoring the Pittsburgh Pirates
January 1972

First, I would like to say I think I have the greatest mother and father that ever lived. I remember when I was a kid, my father and mother had to work from sun to sun to support us kids. And all those years, I think that if anybody suffered to give us kids the best living they could, they did.

Ever since I've been playing baseball, I thank God every day for having made me an athlete. I love and thrive on competition, and that's what has made me work hard every day to keep my mind, my body and my outlook on life at their best.

I think that competition is a great factor in the world today. Great nations such as ours are built on it, and without it man can't achieve much. No competition whatsoever can lead a person or nation to become complacent.

I love competition because when a person is faced with competition, he has to struggle that much harder to be a winner. A winner is proud, and that's the sound foundation on which our nation was built.

One has to work hard for everything he wants today. No one hands it to you on a silver platter. It's a struggle for survival, and no one, with a goal in mind, can afford to let up.

Everyone knows I've been struggling all my life. I believe that every human being is equal, but one has to fight hard all the time to maintain that equality.

I'm from Puerto Rico, but I am an American citizen. I've had the opportunity to do much traveling. I just came back from South Africa and Europe, where I visited many countries. I heard many times that some Americans spit on the American flag. I want to tell you one thing: I wouldn't trade this country for any other country in the world. No matter what, we have the best country in the world—and you'd better believe it!

I'm very proud to be here tonight because last fall we played in the World Series and won it. I always say to myself that we athletes or baseball players are mighty fortunate in many respects. I think that we should pay to the fans to watch us play the game we love. It's a wonderful privilege that we are allowed to play the game we love and make all that money.

Our Pittsburgh Pirates players won the World Series because we pulled together and for each other. We never gave up, even when we had our backs to the wall, and we faced big odds. We thrived on competition, and the harder it became, the harder we fought back. That's why we won the World Series.

❖ ❖ ❖

As you know, time goes so fast. We're living a really fast life. The ones who have children, sometimes we don't have time to see them much. We come back from work, our kids are in bed already. We go back to work, out kids are off to school. We hear a great deal about kids today, how bad some are and that our American youth is rapidly deteriorating.

I think we can do something about solving our mounting difficulties at home. There is nothing wrong with our homes, our country, that a little more care, a little more concern, a little more love, won't cure. We need to show love and to love, not only our kids and our family as a whole but also our neighbors. We're all brothers and sisters, and we must give each other a helping hand when it is needed.

I'm very proud to be a baseball player. As I said before, it is the greatest life. I wouldn't change this life for anything else in the world, and I wouldn't change this country for any other in the world, either. It's the greatest.

- Spring training has two leagues, the Grapefruit League in Florida and the Cactus League in Arizona. The teams play in the league where they train for the season.

- The first documented spring training was in 1888 with the Cincinnati Red Stockings. The owner agreed to a southern tour as it allowed him to weed out the old players and see who was worth keeping.

- Ty Cobb, Jimmie Foxx, and Edd Roush all were known as spring-training holdouts, because they refused to travel with their teams and instead worked out on their own.

- During World War II, baseball scaled back in all areas, including spring training, because most trains were packed with supplies and troops and it seemed frivolous for teams to travel south. Instead, the teams trained close to their home base.

- Most teams were training regularly in Florida by the '40s, but the Giants and the Indians became the first teams to make the shift from Florida to Arizona in 1947, beginning the new Cactus League.

SPRING TRAINING:
CACTUS & GRAPEFRUIT

★ The lampposts at the Phoenix Muni Stadium, spring-training home of the Oakland A's, were originally used at the Polo Grounds in New York.

★ In addition to Florida, the Dodgers have trained in Cuba and the Dominican Republic.

★ The movie *Major League* was filmed at Hi Corbett Field, a onetime spring home to the Cleveland Indians.

★ When William Wrigley, owner of the Chicago Cubs, bought California's Catalina Island in 1919, he began using it as a training ground for his team. From 1921 to 1951, the Cubs used the island's unpaved goat trails for tough workouts as sportswriters sent dispatches to chilly Chicago residents about the sunny adventures of their team.

★ One of the best ways to enjoy a spring-training game is on a "berm"—a grassy area beyond the outfield—offered by stadiums including the Tigers' Joker Marchant Stadium, where fans can bring blankets and watch the game from field level.

★ The Athletics trained only one year outside the Grand Canyon State. In 1968, the A's took up shop in Bradenton, Florida, current spring-training home of the Pirates.

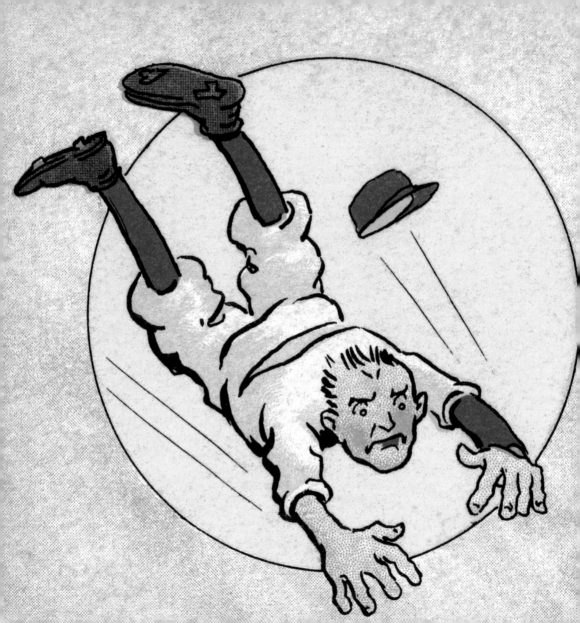

IF GOD WANTED FOOTBALL PLAYED IN THE SPRING, HE WOULD NOT HAVE INVENTED BASEBALL.

—SAM RUTIGLIANO

Ballpark Lemonade

1 ½ cups sugar

6 cups water

1 ½ cups fresh-squeezed lemon juice (about 8 to 10 lemons)

Ice cubes

If you're out at the ballpark or simply tossing the ball around in the backyard, nothing cools off players and fans like a refreshing glass of fresh-squeezed Ballpark Lemonade.

1. Mix the sugar and 2 cups of the water in a large saucepan and bring to a boil.

2. Reduce the heat and simmer, stirring occasionally, until the sugar dissolves.

3. Remove from the heat and cool.

4. Stir the juice into the syrup.

5. Stir the above mixture into the remaining water in a 2 ½-quart container. Refrigerate until cold.

6. Serve in red plastic cups with ice cubes.

Makes 2 quarts.

The Umpire Is a Most Unhappy Man

BY WILL HOUGH & FRANK ADAMS

An umpire is a cross between a bullfrog and a goat,
He has a mouth that's flannel lined and brass tubes in his throat;
He needs a cool and level head, that isn't hard to hit,
So when the fans beat up his frame,
They'll have a nice place to sit;
The only job that's worse, is driver on a hearse.

Chorus:
How'd you like to be an umpire,
Work like his is merely play,
He don't even have to ask for,
All the things that come his way,
When the crowd yells, "knock his block off,"
"Soak him good," says ev'ry fan,
Then who wants to be an umpire,
The brick-bats whiz, when he gets his,
For the umpire is a most unhappy man.

Napoleon and Washington were generals of old,
Their lightest word moved regiments and armies we are told;
Where'er they led men followed them, but only came for hire,
Just think of all that gratis come,
To follow the bold umpire;
He leads them with such vim, because they're chasing him.

BASEBALL IS ALMOST THE ONLY ORDERLY THING IN A VERY UNORDERLY WORLD.

—BILL VEECK

WAIT TILL NEXT YEAR

BY DORIS KEARNS GOODWIN

When I was six, my father gave me a bright-red scorebook that opened my heart to the game of baseball. After dinner on long summer nights, he would sit beside me in our small enclosed porch to hear my account of that day's Brooklyn Dodger game. Night after night he taught me the odd collection of symbols, numbers, and letters that enable a baseball lover to record every action of the game. Our score sheets had blank boxes in which we could draw our own slanted lines in the form of a diamond as we followed players around the bases. Wherever the baserunner's progress stopped, the line stopped. He instructed me to fill in the unused boxes at the end of each inning with an elaborate checkerboard design which made it absolutely clear who had been the last to bat and who would lead off the next inning. By the time I had mastered the art of scorekeeping, a lasting bond had been forged among my father, baseball, and me.

All through the summer of 1949, my first summer as a fan, I spent my afternoons sitting cross-legged before the squat Philco radio which stood as a permanent fixture on our porch in Rockville

Centre, on the South Shore of Long Island, New York. With my scorebook spread before me, I attended Dodger games through the courtly voice of Dodger announcer Red Barber. As he announced the lineup, I carefully printed each player's name in a column on the left side of my sheet. Then, using the standard system my father had taught me, which assigned a number to each position in the field, starting with a "1" for the pitcher and ending with a "9" for the right fielder, I recorded every play. I found it difficult at times to sit still. As the Dodgers came to bat, I would walk around the room, talking to the players as if they were standing in front of me. At critical junctures, I tried to make a bargain, whispering and cajoling while Pee Wee Reese or Duke Snider stepped into the batter's box: "Please, please, get a hit. If you get a hit now, I'll make my bed every day for a week." Sometimes, when the score was close and the opposing team at bat with men on base, I was too agitated to listen. Asking my mother to keep notes, I left the house for a walk around the block, hoping that when I returned the enemy threat would be over, and once again we'd be up at bat. Mostly, however, I stayed at my post, diligently recording each inning so that, when my father returned from his job as bank examiner for the State of New York, I could re-create for him the game he had missed.

When my father came home from the city, he would change from his three-piece suit into long pants and a short-sleeved sport shirt, and come downstairs for the ritual Manhattan cocktail with my mother. Then my parents would summon me for dinner from my play on the street outside our house. All through dinner I had to restrain myself from telling him about the day's game, waiting for the special time to come when we would sit together on the couch, my scorebook on my lap.

"Well, did anything interesting happen today?" he would begin. And even before the daily question was completed I had eagerly launched into my narrative of every play, and almost every pitch, of that afternoon's contest. It never crossed my mind to wonder if, at the close of a day's work, he might find my lengthy account the least bit tedious. For there was mastery as well as pleasure in our nightly ritual. Through my knowledge, I commanded my father's undivided attention, the sign of his love. It would instill in me an early awareness of the power of narrative, which would introduce a lifetime of storytelling, fueled by the naive confidence that others would find me as entertaining as my father did.

Michael Francis Aloysius Kearns, my father, was a short man who appeared much larger on account of his erect bearing, broad chest, and thick neck. He had a ruddy Irish complexion, and his green eyes flashed with humor and vitality. When he smiled his entire face was transformed, radiating enthusiasm and friendliness. He called me "Bubbles," a pet name he had chosen, he told me, because I seemed to enjoy so many things. Anxious to confirm his description, I refused to let my enthusiasm wane, even when I grew tired or grumpy. Thus excitement about things became a habit, a part of my personality, and the expectation that I should enjoy new experiences often engendered the enjoyment itself.

These nightly recountings of the Dodgers' progress provided my first lessons in the narrative art. From the scorebook, with its tight squares of neatly arranged symbols, I could unfold the tale of an entire game and tell a story that seemed to last almost as long as the game itself. At first, I was unable to resist the temptation to skip ahead to an important play in later innings. At times, I grew so excited about a Dodger victory that I blurted out the final score before I had hardly begun. But as I became more experienced in my storytelling, I learned to build a dramatic story with a beginning, middle, and end. Slowly, I learned that if I could recount the game, one batter at a time, inning by inning, without divulging the out-come, I could keep the suspense and my father's interest alive until the very last pitch. Sometimes I pretended that I was the great Red Barber himself, allowing my voice to swell when reporting a home run, quieting to a whisper when the action grew tense, injecting tid-bits about the players into my reports. At critical moments, I would jump from the couch to illustrate a ball that turned foul at the last moment or a dropped fly that was scored as an error.

"How many hits did Roy Campanella get?" my dad would ask. Tracing my finger across the horizontal line that represented Campanella's at-bats that day, I would count. "One, two, three. Three hits, a single, a double, and another single." "How many strikeouts for Don Newcombe?" It was easy. I would count the K's. "One, two . . . eight. He had eight strikeouts." Then he'd ask me more subtle questions about different plays—whether a strikeout was called or swinging, whether the double play was around the horn, whether the single that won the game was hit to left or right. If I had scored carefully, using the elaborate system he had taught me, I would know the answers. My father pointed to the second inning, where Jackie Robinson had hit a single and then stolen second. There was excitement in his voice. "See, it's all here. While Robinson was dancing off second, he rattled the pitcher so badly that the next two guys walked to load the bases. That's the impact Robinson makes, game after game. Isn't he something?" His smile at such moments inspired me to take my responsibility seriously.

Sometimes, a particular play would trigger in my father a memory of a similar situation in a game when he was young, and he would tell me stories about the Dodgers when he was a boy growing up in Brooklyn. His vivid tales featured strange heroes such as Casey Stengel, Zack Wheat, and Jimmy Johnston. Though it was hard at first to imagine that the Casey

Stengel I knew, the manager of the Yankees, with his colorful language and hilarious antics, was the same man as the Dodger outfielder who hit an inside-the-park home run at the first game ever played at Ebbets Field, my father so skillfully stitched together the past and the present that I felt as if I were living in different time zones. If I closed my eyes, I imagined I was at Ebbets Field in the 1920s for that celebrated game when Dodger right fielder Babe Herman hit a double with the bases loaded, and through a series of mishaps on the base paths, three Dodgers ended up at third base at the same time. And I was sitting by my father's side, five years before I was born, when the lights were turned on for the first time at Ebbets Field, the crowd gasping and then cheering as the summer night was transformed into startling day.

When I had finished describing the game, it was time to go to bed, unless I could convince my father to tally each player's batting average, reconfiguring his statistics to reflect the developments of that day's game. If Reese went 3 for 5 and had started the day at .303, my father showed me, by adding and multiplying all the numbers in his head, that his average would rise to .305. If Snider went 0 for 4 and started the day at .301, then his average would dip four points below the .300 mark. If Carl Erskine had let in three runs in seven innings, then my father would multiply three times nine, divide that by the number of innings pitched, and magically tell me whether Erskine's earned-run average had improved or worsened. It was this facility with numbers that had made it possible for my father to pass the civil-service test and become a bank examiner despite leaving school after the eighth grade. And this job had carried him from a Brooklyn tenement to a house with a lawn on Southard Avenue in Rockville Centre.

All through that summer, my father kept from me the knowledge that running box scores appeared in the daily newspapers. He never mentioned that these abbreviated histories had been a staple feature of the sports pages since the nineteenth century and were generally the first thing he and his fellow commuters turned to when they opened the *Daily News* and the *Herald Tribune* in the morning. I believed that, if I did not recount the games he had missed, my father would never have been able to follow our Dodgers the proper way, day by day, play by play, inning by inning. In other words, without me, his love of baseball would be forever unfulfilled.

Ebbets Field, Brooklyn, New York

As I grew up, I knew that as a building (Fenway Park) was on the level of Mount Olympus, the Pyramid at Giza, the nation's Capitol, the Czar's Winter Palace, and the Louvre—except, of course, that it is better than all those inconsequential places.

—A. Bartlett Giamatti

GREAT MOMENTS
IN BASEBALL PART II

April 8, 1974 Hank Aaron blasts his record-breaking 715th career home run during the fourth inning of the Braves' home opener against the Los Angeles Dodgers.

October 21, 1975 Carlton Fisk of the Red Sox leads off the bottom of the twelfth with a home run, which he frantically waves off the left-field foul pole at Fenway Park during Game 6 of the World Series, giving Boston a 7–6 victory over the Cincinnati Reds.

October 14, 1976 Yankee Chris Chambliss hits a homer in the bottom of the ninth to secure the win over Kansas City, making the Yankees the American League Champions for the first time since 1964. Fans at Yankee Stadium are so excited, they pour onto the field in such numbers that Chambliss needs a police escort to make it to home plate.

October 18, 1977 "Mr. October," Reggie Jackson, slams three home runs into the Yankee Stadium bleachers during Game 6 of the World Series.

September 11, 1985 In front of a sold-out Riverfront Stadium, Pete Rose of the Cincinnati Reds hits a line drive in the first inning, bringing his all-time hit count to 4,192 to top Ty Cobb as the king of hits.

October 15, 1988 During Game 1 of the World Series, an injured Kirk Gibson comes up to pinch-hit in the ninth inning with his Dodgers trailing the Oakland A's 4–3. He knocks a two-run homer into the Dodger Stadium stands.

May 1, 1991 Ranger Nolan Ryan pitches his seventh career no-hitter against the Blue Jays at the age of 44.

320

715

October 26, 1991 In Game Six of the World Series, the Twins trail the Braves three games to two when Kirby Puckett makes a leaping catch, forcing the game into extra innings. Puckett goes on to end the game with an 11th inning home run.

September 6, 1995 Cal Ripken, Jr. plays his 2,131st consecutive game for the Baltimore Orioles, breaking Lou Gehrig's "unbreakable record" (below).

October 27, 2004 The Red Sox beat the Curse and the Cardinals to win their first World Series Championship since 1918.

October 26, 2005 The White Sox beat their Curse and the Astros to win their first World Series Championship since 1917.

Dream of a Hanging Curve

Norbert Krapf

When I see it spinning
like a Florida grapefruit
toward me, let me not
lunge at it like a rookie.

It it's outside, help me
shift my weight and lash
it to the opposite field.

If it should come down
the middle, let me send it
right back where it came
from, but harder and faster.

If it comes toward the inside corner,
give me the patience to wait,

turn on it, and pull it down
the line to kick up chalk
and carom around in the corner.

If I should have the luck
to make the right connection,
follow through perfectly
and see the ball rise
in an arc that will end
somewhere behind the fence,
let me not take too long
to circle the bases, gesture
toward the other dugout,
jump onto home plate,
or high-five everyone in sight
while the pitcher hangs his head.

Baltimore Orioles' Crab Cakes

1 pound crab meat

½ cup dry breadcrumbs

1 egg, beaten

1 tablespoon mayonnaise

1 teaspoon prepared Dijon-style mustard

1 teaspoon Worcestershire sauce

1 tablespoon Old Bay Seasoning

1 teaspoon parsley

2 tablespoons butter

No two things say Baltimore more than crab cakes and the Orioles. At Camden Yards, baseball fans can enjoy one of the most beautiful ballparks in the country along with tasty seafood cakes at restaurants like Past Times. When you want to whip up your own taste of Baltimore, try these crab cakes, perfect for any late game snack.

1. In a medium-size bowl, combine the breadcrumbs and the crab meat. Stir the beaten egg, mayonnaise, mustard, Worcestershire and Old Bay Seasoning. Lightly mix these ingredients, being careful not to overwork the crab meat.

2. Form into 8 round, flat crab cakes.

3. Heat butter in a skillet over medium heat. Fry the cakes on each side until crusty and golden brown. Serve warm.

Serves 4.

I BELIEVE IN THE RIP VAN WINKLE THEORY: THAT A MAN FROM 1910 MUST BE ABLE TO WAKE UP AFTER BEING ASLEEP FOR SEVENTY YEARS, WALK INTO A BALLPARK AND UNDERSTAND BASEBALL PERFECTLY.

—BOWIE KUHN

VIVA EL BÉISBOL:
THE LATIN FACTOR

★ Baseball arrived in Cuba in 1864 with Nemesio Guilló, a young Cuban who returned from studying in America with a bat and ball. He and his brother founded the Habana Base Ball Club.

★ In Cuba, amateur leagues used to be organized around the local sugar mills.

★ Initially, baseball was seen as a way to rebel against the Spanish tradition of bullfighting and so was embraced by the young and working class.

★ The first Latino in professional baseball was Esteban Enrique Bellán, who joined the Troy Haymakers in 1869. Bellán was born in 1850 in Cuba and played three years as an infielder.

★ In the early days, a few "white" Latinos were able to break into the majors, while "black" Latinos were not. The most notable Latino player during this time was the Cincinnati Reds' Adolfo Luque (the Pride of Havana), who was an outstanding pitcher for 20 years with a lifetime record of 193 wins and 179 losses.

★ The first Puerto Rican to play professionally in the United States was Hiram Bithorn, who made his debut in 1942. He pitched four years for the Chicago Cubs and White Sox with a record of 34 wins and 31 losses. The current baseball stadium in San Juan is named after him.

★ Orestes "Minnie" Miñoso was the first black Latino player to enter the major leagues, in 1949. He played for the Cleveland Indians.

★ Miñoso played for 17 years in the majors and was a three-time league leader in stolen bases. He is the only player in history to have played in the major leagues during five different decades.

Orestes "Minnie" Miñosa with the Cleveland Indians.

☆ When Castro took control in Cuba, the country became the biggest supplier of major league baseball players outside the United States. In 1950 alone, six pitchers from Cuba were sent to play for the Washington Senators.

☆ After the Cuban Revolution, one of the first freedoms Castro took from Cubans was the right to play professional baseball, in 1959.

☆ Tony Oliva was the only player in the history of the majors to win batting crowns in his first two full seasons in the big leagues.

☆ Pittsburgh Pirate Roberto Clemente was discovered in San Juan while still in high school. Before he died in a tragic plane crash on his way to offer humanitarian aid in Nicaragua, he won the National League batting championship, was awarded twelve Gold Gloves, and was the MVP in the 1971 World Series.

- Jose Canseco hit at least 30 home runs and drove in at least 100 runs in his first three seasons, something no one else did in the 20th century. In 1988, he stole 40 bases and hit 40 homers, another feat never before achieved. He was also the first player to earn $5 million in a single season.

- Major-league teams in Mexico must negotiate with the Mexican League team for a player they are interested in, instead of just with the player. This is the main reason why so few major leaguers hail from Mexico as compared with other Latin countries.

- As an interim manager for the St. Louis Cardinals in 1938, Miguel Angel Gonzalez became the first Latino manager in the majors.

- In Venezuela and many other countries, shortstop is a coveted position thanks to the legacy of great Latino shortstops, including Dave Concepción, Chico Carrasquel, Luis Aparicio, and Omar Vizquel.

- Martín Dihigo was the first Latin American to be elected into the Hall of Fame, even though during his time he was forced to play in the Negro Leagues and in the Carribean due to his dark skin.

- Some great Latino players through the years have been immortalized in the National Baseball Hall of Fame, including Roberto Clemente, Luis Aparicio, Al López, Rod Carew, "Lefty" Gómez, Martín Dihigo, and Juan Marichal.

- The 13 Latino countries represented in the major leagues have now sent more than 750 ballplayers to America.

- Orlando "El Duque" Hernández followed his brother Liván in defecting from Cuba in 1997 to play baseball in America. Other Cuban defectors in the majors include Tony Pérez, Tony Oliva, and Rolando Arrojo.

TRYING TO SNEAK A PITCH PAST HANK AARON IS LIKE TRYING TO SNEAK THE SUNRISE PAST A ROOSTER.

—JOE ADCOCK

333

TAKE ME OUT TO THE BALLPARK

BY BILL BRYSON

People sometimes ask me, "What is the difference between baseball and cricket?"

The answer is simple. Both are games of great skill involving balls and bats but with this crucial difference: Baseball is exciting, and when you go home at the end of the day you know who won.

I'm joking, of course. Cricket is a wonderful sport, full of deliciously scattered micromoments of real action. If a doctor ever instructs me to take a complete rest and not get overexcited, I shall become a fan at once. In the meantime, my heart belongs to baseball.

It's what I grew up with, what I played as a boy, and that of course is vital to any meaningful appreciation of a sport. I had this brought home to me many years ago in England when I went out on a soccer ground with a couple of English friends to knock a ball around.

I had watched soccer on television and thought I had a fair idea of what was required, so when one of them lofted a ball in my direction, I decided to flick it casually into the net with my head, the way I had seen Kevin Keegan do it on TV. I thought that it would be like heading a beachball—that there would be a gentle, airy *ponk* sound and that the ball would lightly leave my brow and drift in a pleasing arc into the net. But of course it was like heading a bowling ball. I have never felt anything so startlingly not like I expected it to feel. I walked around for four hours on wobbly legs with a big red circle and the word "MITRE" imprinted on my forehead and vowed never again to do anything so foolish and painful.

I bring this up here because the World Series has just started, and I want you to know why I am very excited about it. The World Series, I should perhaps explain, is the annual baseball contest between the champion of the American League and the champion of the National League.

Actually, that's not quite true because they changed the system some years ago. The trouble with the old way of doing things was that it involved only two teams. Now, you don't have to be a brain surgeon to work out that if you could somehow contrive to include more teams there would be a lot more money in the thing.

So each league divided itself into three divisions of four or five teams each. So now the World Series is not the contest between the two best teams in baseball—at least not necessarily—but rather between the winners of a series of playoff games involving the Western, Eastern, and Central divisional champions of each league, plus (and this was particularly inspired, I think) a pair of "wild card" teams that didn't win anything at all.

It is all immensely complicated, but essentially it means that practically every team in baseball except the Chicago Cubs gets a chance to go to the World Series.

The Chicago Cubs don't get to go because they never manage to qualify even under a system as magnificently accommodating as this. Often they *almost* qualify, and sometimes they are in such a commanding position that you cannot believe they won't qualify, but always in the end they doggedly manage to come up short. Whatever it takes—losing seventeen games in a row, letting easy balls go through their legs, crashing comically into each other in the outfield—you can be certain the Cubs will manage it.

They have been doing this, reliably and efficiently, for over half a century. They haven't been in a World Series since 1945. Stalin had good years more recently than that. This heartwarming annual failure by the Cubs is almost the only thing in baseball that hasn't changed in my lifetime, and I appreciate that very much.

It's not easy being a baseball fan because baseball fans are a hopelessly sentimental bunch, and there is no room for sentiment in something as wildly lucrative as an American sport. For anyone from outside America, one of the most remarkable aspects of American sports is how casually franchises abandon their loyal fans and move to a new city. In English soccer, it would be unthinkable for, say, Manchester United to move to London or Everton to find a new home in Portsmouth, or anyone to go anywhere really, but here that sort of thing happens all the time, sometimes more than once. The Braves began life in Boston, then moved to Milwaukee, then moved to Atlanta. The A's started in Philadelphia, then switched to Kansas City, then pushed on to Oakland.

Meanwhile, the Major Leagues have repeatedly expanded to where they have reached the point where it is deucedly hard, for me at any rate, to keep track of it all. Of the thirty teams in Major League baseball, just eleven are where they were when I was a kid.

There are teams out there now that I know nothing about. Without looking at the standings, I couldn't tell you whether the Arizona Diamondbacks are in the National League or the American League. That's a terrifying confession for someone who loves the game.

Even when teams stay put, they don't actually stay put. I mean by this that they are constantly tearing down old stadiums to build new ones. Call me eccentric, call me fastidious, but I truly believe that baseball should only be watched in an old stadium. It used to be that every big American city had a venerable ballpark. Generally these were dank and creaky, but they had character. You would get splinters from the seats, the soles of your shoes would congeal to the floor from all the years of sticky stuff that had been spilled during exciting moments, and your view would inevitably be obscured by a cast-iron column supporting the roof. But that was all part of the glory.

Only four of these old parks are left, and two of them—Yankee Stadium in New York and Fenway Park in Boston—are under threat. I won't say that Fenway's relative nearness was the decisive consideration in our settling in New Hampshire, but it was certainly a factor. Now the owners want to tear it down and build a new stadium.

In fairness it must be said that the new ballparks of the 1990s, as opposed to the multipurpose arenas built in the previous thirty years, do strive to keep the character and intimacy of the old ballparks—sometimes even improve on them—but they have one inescapable, irremediable flaw. They are new. They have no history, no connection with a glorious and continuous past. No matter how scrupulous a new Fenway they build, it won't be the place where Ted Williams batted. It won't make your feet stick. It won't echo in the same way. It won't smell funny. It won't be Fenway.

I keep saying that I won't go to the new park when they finally raze Fenway, but I know I'm lying because I am hopelessly addicted to the game. All of which increases my almost boundless respect and admiration for the hapless Chicago Cubs. To their credit, the Cubs have never threatened to leave Chicago and continue to play at Wrigley Field. They even still play mostly day games—the way God intended baseball to be played. A day game at Wrigley Field is one of the great American experiences.

And here's the problem. Nobody deserves to go to the World Series more than the Chicago Cubs. But they can't go because that would spoil their custom of never going. It is an irreconcilable paradox.

You see what I mean when I say that it is not easy being a baseball fan?

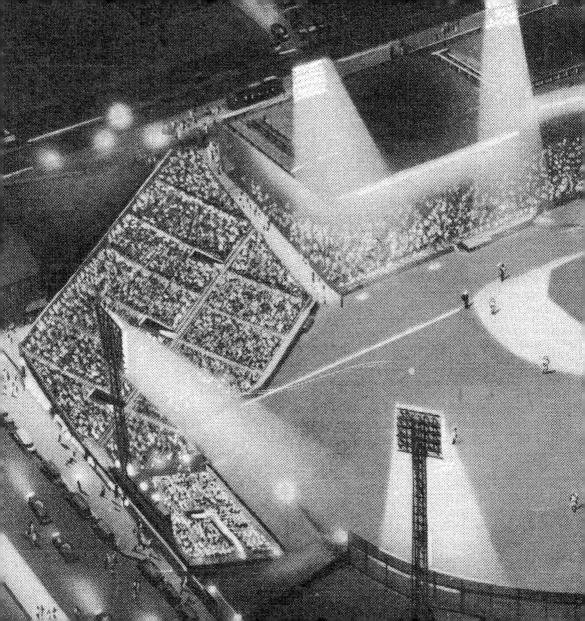

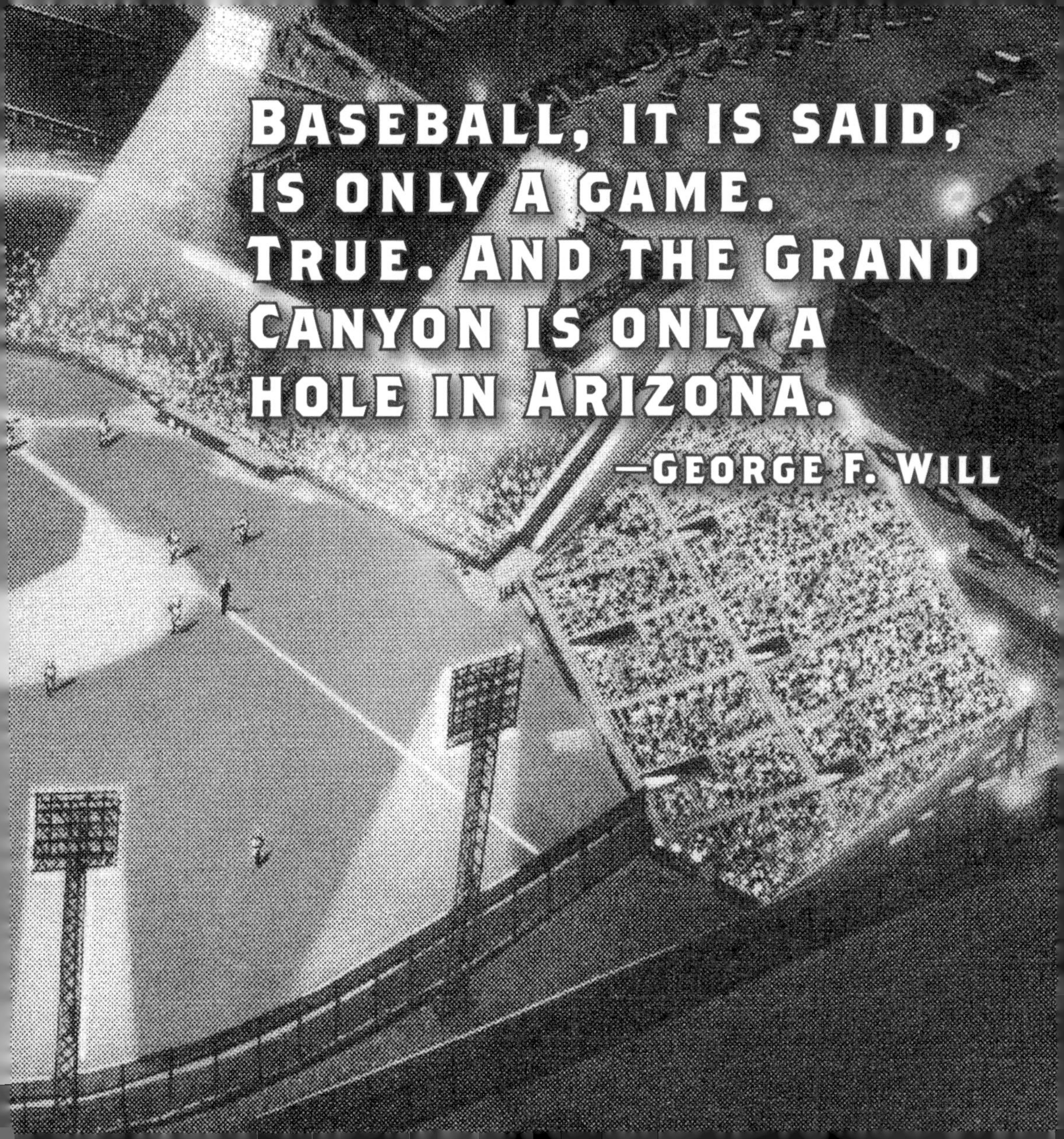
BASEBALL, IT IS SAID,
IS ONLY A GAME.
TRUE. AND THE GRAND
CANYON IS ONLY A
HOLE IN ARIZONA.
—GEORGE F. WILL

LANGUAGE OUT OF LEFT FIELD:
BASEBALL VERNACULAR

around the horn, *n.* a double play that starts at third base, continues to second, and ends at first.

backdoor slider, *n.* a pitch that seems to be out of the strike zone until the last moment, when it swings back over the plate.

back-to-back jacks, *n.* when two home runs are hit one after another in a single inning.

balk, *n., v., intj.* an illegal motion by a pitcher when one or more runners are on base. Intended to keep the pitcher from deceiving runners.

Bermuda triangle, *n.* the outfield area where a fly ball cannot be reached by fielders.

Captain Hook, *n.* the nickname of manager Sparky Anderson, who replaced pitchers on the mound regularly. The term now refers to any manager following the same practice.

cheese, *n.* a fastball. Also known as **cannon ball**, **dead red**, **hummer**, **blazer**, **old number one**, **radio ball**.

dead fish, *n.* a pitch thrown with little speed. Also called **dead mackerel** or **salad**.

forty-forty club, *n.* a group of players who have hit forty home runs and stolen forty bases in one season.

ground rules, *n.* rules for a specific field that apply in circumstances not covered by the regular rules of baseball.

ham and eggs, *n.* an easy ground ball that ends in a double play.

inning eater, *n.* a pitcher with endurance.

junkball pitcher, *n.* a pitcher who relies on a variety of pitches to succeed.

meatball, *n.* a pitch that is easy to hit, straight down the middle.

southpaw, *n.* a player who throws with his left arm.

squeeze, *v.* a bunt by the batter that allows the third-base runner to score.

sweet spot, *n.* a section on a baseball bat that players attempt to connect with the ball; it transfers the maximum possible power.

table setter, *n.* a batter, typically in the top of the order, whose goal is to get on base so that other players may drive him home.

365

Jack Buck

When someone asks you your favorite sport
And you answer Baseball in a blink
There are certain qualities you must possess
And you're more attached than you think.
In the frozen grip of winter
I'm sure you'll agree with me
Not a day goes by without someone
Talking baseball to some degree.
The calendar flips on New Year's Day
The Super Bowl comes and it goes
Get the other sports out of the way
The green grass and the fever grows.
It's time to pack a bag and take a trip
To Arizona or the Sunshine State
Perhaps you can't go, but there's the radio
So you listen-you root-you wait.
They start the campaign, pomp and pageantry reign
You claim the pennant on Opening Day

From April till fall
You follow the bouncing white ball
Your team is set to go all the way.
They fall short of the series
You have a case of the "wearies"
And need as break from the game
But when Christmas bells jingle
You feel that old tingle
And you're ready for more of the same.
It will be hot dogs for dinner
Six months of heaven, a winner
Yes, Baseball has always been it.
You would amaze all your friends
If they knew to what ends
You'd go for a little old hit.
The best times you're had
Have been with your Mom and your Dad
And a bat and a ball and a glove.
From the first time you played
Till the last time you prayed
It's been a simple matter of love.

SHOELESS JOE

BY W. P. KINSELLA

They'll walk out to the bleacher and sit in shirtsleeves in the perfect evening, or they'll find they have reserved seats somewhere in the grandstand or along one of the baselines—wherever they sat when they were children and cheered their heroes, in whatever park it was, whatever leaf-shaded town in Maine, or Ohio, or California. They'll watch the game, and it will be as if they have knelt in front of a faith healer, or dipped themselves in magic waters where a saint once rose like a serpent and cast benedictions to the wind like peach petals.

The memories will be so thick that the outfielders will have to brush them away from their faces: squarish cars parked around a frame schoolhouse, blankets covering the engine blocks; Christmas carols drifting like tinseled birds toward the golden wash of the Northern Lights; women shelling peas in linoleum-floored kitchens, cradling the unshelled pods in brindled aprons, tearing open corn husks and waiting for the thrill of the cool sweet scent; apple cheeked children and collie dogs; the coffee-and-oil smell of a general store; people gliding

over the snow
in an open cutter;
the dazzling smell
of horsehide blankets
teasing the senses.

I don't have to tell
you that the one constant
through all the years has been
baseball. America has been erased
like a blackboard, only to be rebuilt and
then erased again. But baseball has marked
time while America has rolled by like a
procession of steamrollers. It is the same game
that Moonlight Graham played in 1905. It is
a living part of history, like calico dresses,
stone crockery, and threshing crews eating at
outdoor tables. It continually reminds us of
what once was, like an Indian-head penny in
a handful of new coins.

347

Joltin' Joe DiMaggio

BY BEN HOMER & ALAN COURTNEY

Hello Joe, whatta you know?
We need a hit so here I go.
Ball one (Yea!)
Ball two (Yea!)
Strike one (Booo!)
Strike two (Kill that umpire!)
A case of Wheaties

He started baseball's famous streak
That's got us all aglow
He's just a man and not a freak,
Joltin' Joe DiMaggio.

Joe, Joe DiMaggio
We want you on our side

He tied the mark at forty-four
July the 1st you know
Since then he's hit a good twelve more
Joltin' Joe DiMaggio

Joe, Joe DiMaggio
We want you on our side

From coast to coast that's all you'll hear
Of Joe the one man show
He's glorified the horsehide sphere
Joltin' Joe DiMaggio

Joe, Joe DiMaggio
We want you on our side

He'll live in baseball's Hall of Fame
He got there blow by blow
Our kids will tell their kids his name
Joltin' Joe DiMaggio

We dream of Joey with the light brown plaque
Joe, Joe DiMaggio
We want you on our side

And now they speak in whispers low
Of how they stopped our Joe
One night in Cleveland Oh Oh Oh
Goodbye streak DiMaggio

Joltin' Joe DiMaggio

NINETY FEET BETWEEN BASES IS PERHAPS AS CLOSE AS MAN HAS EVER COME TO PERFECTION.

—RED SMITH

TEXT CREDITS:

"The Interior Stadium," copyright © 1971 by Roger Angell, from *The Summer Game* by Roger Angell. Used by permission of Viking Penguin, a division of Penguin Putnam, Inc.; "Our National Pastime," from *Dave Barry is from Mars and Venus* by Dave Barry, copyright © 1997 by Dave Barry. Used by permission of Crown Publishers, a division of Random House, Inc.; "Take Me Out to the Ballgame" from *I'm a Stranger Here Myself* by Bill Bryson, copyright © 1999 by Bill Bryson. Used by permission of Broadway Books, a division of Random House, Inc.; "Baseball and Football" from *Braindroppings* by George Carlin. Copyright © 1997 Comedy Concepts, Inc. Reprinted by Permission of Hyperion. All rights reserved; "Catfish" by Bob Dylan. Copyright © 1975 by Ram's Horn Music. All rights reserved. International copyright secured. Reprinted by permission; "The Green Fields of the Mind" by A. Bartlett Giamatti, first published in the *Yale Alumni Magazine*, 11/77. Copyright © 1977 by A. Bartlett Giamatti; Excerpt from *Wait Till Next Year* by Doris Kearns Goodwin reprinted with the permission of Simon & Schuster Adult Publishing Group. Copyright © 1997 by Blithedale Productions, Inc. All rights reserved; "Louisville Slugger" from *Cheeseburgers* by Bob Greene, reprinted with permission of Scribner, a Division of Simon & Schuster Adult Publishing Group. Copyright © 1985 by John Deadline Enterprises, Inc. All rights reserved; "Instruction" by Conrad Hilberry. Reprinted with permission of author; "The Umpire is a Most Unhappy Man" by Will Hough and Frank Adams. Used by the permission of Jerry Vogel Music and Charles K. Harris Music; "Brooklyns Lose" by William Hueman. Originally published in *Sports Illustrated*, 1954; Excerpt from *Shoeless Joe* by W.P. Kinsella copyright © 1982 by W.P. Kinsella. Reprinted by permission of Houghton Mifflin Company and Carolyn Swayze. All rights reserved; "Dream of a Hanging Curve" from *The Country I Come From* (Archer Books, 2002), © 1999 by Norbert Krapf. Used with permission; Excerpt from *Summer of '98: When Homers Flew, Records Fell, and Baseball Reclaimed America* by Mike Lupica. Copyright © 1999 by Mike Lupica. Used by permission of Penguin Putnam, Inc.; Excerpt from *The Natural* by Bernard Malamud, copyright © 1952, renewed 1980 by Bernard Malamud. Reprinted by permission of Farrar, Straus and Giroux, LLC; Excerpt from *Notes of a Baseball Dreamer: A Memoir* by Robert Mayer. Copyright © 2003 by Robert Mayer. Reprinted by permission of Houghton Mifflin Company. All rights reserved; "The Kid" by E. Ethelbert Miller from *First Light: New and Selected Poems*, Baltimore, Black Classic Press. Copyright © 1994. Reprinted with permission of author; "Line-up for Yesterday" copyright © 1949 by Ogden Nash. Reprinted by permission of Curtis Brown, Ltd.; "A Matter of Record" reprinted with the permission of HarperCollins from *One for the Record* by George Plimpton. Copyright © 1974; "There Used to be a Ballpark" by Joe Raposo. © 1973 Hal Leonard and Warner Brothers Music; Reprinted courtesy of *Sports Illustrated*; "Hot to Trot With No Place to Go" by Rick Reilly, May 11, 1998, Copyright © 1998. Time Inc, All rights reserved; Excerpt from *Bull Durham* by Ron Shelton. © 1988 Orion Pictures Corporation; "It Was a Great Day in Jersey" by Wendell Smith from *Pittsburgh Courier*, April 19, 1946. Copyright © 1946, reprinted by permission of Wyonella Smith; "Right Field" by Willy Welch, copyright © 1987, Playing Right Music, 9430 Springwater, Dallas, TX 75228. Used by the permission of Willy Welch.

ART CREDITS:

Pgs. 1, 100: J. F. Kernan; Pg. 19: Bob Olen; Pgs. 24, 25, 26, 61, 62, 94, 122, 288, 295, 309, 320, 329: National Baseball Hall of Fame Library, Cooperstown, NY; Pg. 40: Ronald McLeod; Pg. 46: Gene Carr; Pg. 77: R.F. Outcault; Pg. 84: Frank Snapro; Pg. 91: H. M. Rose; Pg. 134: "100th Anniversary of Baseball" by Norman Rockwell. Printed by permission of the Norman Rockwell Family Agency. Copyright © 1939 the Norman Rockwell Family Entities; Pg. 150: Jang Campbell; Pg. 156: E. Madcliff; Pg. 162: Norman Hall; Pg. 176: Robert Riggs; Pg. 187: Arthur Crouch; Pgs. 212, 300: S. Bergman; Pg. 234: H. Seaton; Pg. 238: W. E. Ayres; Pg. 273: Jeanne Bendick; Pg. 303: Alan Foster; Pg. 316: Frank E. Cooper; Pg. 343: Torry Roy; Pg. 344: J. Johnson

Published in 2006 by Welcome Books
An imprint of Welcome Enterprises, Inc.
6 West 18th Street, New York, NY 10011
Tel: 212-989-3200; Fax: 212-989-3205
www.welcomebooks.com

Publisher: Lena Tabori
Designer: Jon Glick
Project Manager: Natasha Tabori Fried
Editorial Assistants: Maren Elizabeth Gregerson, Jeffrey Scott McCord

Additional assistance provided by Eric Nelson Norgaard and his prolific baseball library.

Copyright © 2006 Welcome Enterprises, Inc.

All rights reserved. No parts of this book may be reproduced in any form or by any means, electronic or mechanical, including photocopying or by any information storage or retrieval system, without permission in writing from the publisher.

Library of Congress Cataloging-in-Publication Data on file.

13-ISBN 978-1-932183-91-7
10-ISBN 1-932183-91-4

Printed in China

First Edition

10 9 8 7 6 5 4 3 2 1

352